The Dog MEOWS, The Cat BARKS

PRAISE FOR EKA KURNIAWAN

Beauty is a Wound

'Kurniawan…is in many ways a literary child of Günter Grass, Gabriel García Márquez, and Salman Rushdie.'

—*The New York Review of Books*

'Original and powerful…Maybe, who knows, the judges of the Nobel Prize could, in a few years, consider giving [Eka] the prize that Indonesia has never received?'

—*Le Monde*

'A glorious melange of comic grotesquery, romance and political satire… Kurniawan is a tremendously exciting and promising writer, and one who in years to come might even provide a long-overdue replacement for Pramoedyan Anata Toer as the automatic point of comparison for any new Indonesian literature appearing in translation.'

—Tim Hannigan, *Asian Review of Books*

Man Tiger

Longlisted for the Man Booker International Prize for Fiction 2016

'[*Man Tiger*'s] explosive prose and provocative employment of fantastical elements will startle any reader.'

—*Huffington Post*

'Tight, focused and thrilling. Like a good crime novel, *Man Tiger* works best when read in a single sitting, and its propulsive suspense is all the more remarkable because Kurniawan reveals both victim and murderer in the first sentence.'

—*New York Times Book Review*

'A slim, wry story…at once elegant and bawdy, experimental, and political.'

—*The LA Review of Books*

Vengeance is Mine, All Others Pay Cash

'Exuberant, funny, crackling with energy and invention.'

—*The Times, London*

'This wild and enthralling novel manages to entertain while offering readers insight into the traditions of a little-known South East Asian culture. Kurniawan has officially put the West on notice.'

—*Publishers Weekly*

Kitchen Curse: Stories

'These stories show how we are laid bare to the chaos, mysteries and powers of all kinds of other beings, and how we have always continued to resist, and to simply live.'

—Khairani Barokka, author of *Rope*

The Dog MEOWS, The Cat BARKS

Eka Kurniawan

Translated by **Annie Tucker**

SPEAKING TIGER

SPEAKING TIGER BOOKS
125A, Ground Floor, Shahpur Jat, near Asiad Village,
New Delhi 110049

First published in Indonesian by PT Gramedia Pustaka Utama, Jakarta 2024
First published in India by Speaking Tiger Books 2026

This English translation courtesy New Directions Publishing USA

ISBN: 978-93-6336-415-8

10 9 8 7 6 5 4 3 2 1

Typeset in Crimson Text by
SÜRYA, New Delhi

Printed at PRINTWORKS, New Delhi, India

I STOPPED GOING TO MOSQUE. I NO LONGER JOINED IN WORSHIP. I never said my prayers before bed. Sato Reang eats with his left hand—so stupid—and barges in where he pleases, without calling out a greeting. If I was feeling lazy, I'd just piss on a banana tree, and I wouldn't wash myself off after.

No lightning struck me like a fire whip from the beyond. No earthquake came to knock my house down. No dog lunged out of nowhere to sink its teeth into my calf. Sato Reang eats his fill. He laughs heartily at the craziest jokes. He sleeps soundly, like a felled tree trunk, and wakes up fresh-faced and shining. Of course he occasionally suffers from some small annoyance, like an itchy ass-hole, but that's easily fixed with cheap ointment from the village store.

'Come on, Jamal, commit one teeny tiny sin,' I cajoled my schoolmate, proselytizing my newfound enlightenment. 'You're a pious kid. You've earned so many heavenly rewards—a big old pile of them! No amount of sin could ever make even a dent.'

Jamal mumbled a prayer under his breath for God's protection.

That tickled me and I was about to laugh, but he looked at me as if he were seeing a demon. And I was happy he did—at least *someone* no longer saw me as a little kid being driven around on a bicycle, hiding his face in his father's back on a Saturday night. I didn't need to hide my face anymore. They could go ahead and take a good look at my nose, wide and slightly upturned, my thick dark lips, my thin eyebrows arched over my eyes—and see the face of Satan there. How marvellous, I thought. Truly, Sato Reang has transformed. And I would never let anyone change my life back to how it used to be.

'It's no big deal if you skip your prayers once in a while,' I continued, virtuous but a tad intractable, in the mode of a master preacher. 'If the angels happen to inquire, you can tell them you've already prayed thousands of times, and that would be the truth.'

Jamal paled in disbelief and went back to his mumbling, begging for God's protection, this time with clarification: from the temptations of accursed Satan. Ha! I was a little satan!

Plenty of our classmates blew off worship—the feet of a few of them had not touched a mosque floor since they were very small—but no one had ever suggested Jamal should do the same.

It was the second recess, when a handful of kids would go to the mosque behind the school for their midday prayers. Just like he used to, Jamal had approached me and invited me to go there with him. But this time I'd said, 'Nah, I don't feel like it.' I could have easily anticipated his shock—he never would've expected such a thing to come out of my mouth—but at that very moment an unexpected glimmer of an idea appeared in my mind and took hold of me, and suddenly became my life mission, or at least, a goal of sorts for the time I had left at school.

I decided to liberate Jamal. Entice him to sample some worldly pleasures. Show him that there was more to life than just worship and reciting holy verse. Deep down, I was sure he must be hearing the sound of his father's machete hacking his soccer ball in two. Or seeing his stuffed monkey set on fire. Or maybe his fear took some other form, but nevertheless I was overcome with pity, because he still had a father and a grandfather to deal with. 'I feel sorry for you, Jamal,' I said. 'But listen, your father won't know whether or not you've said your prayers.'

He didn't react at first, trying to process what I was saying. Then he opened his mouth and out came a whisper, so soft I could barely hear, 'You're the one to feel sorry for, Sato. You and your father. Truly. Your poor father.'

But that just made me all the more determined. Jamal would become a little devil like me. I would make sure of it.

OF COURSE, JUST LIKE MOST LITTLE KIDS, LONG BEFORE ALL THIS I went to mosque and studied prayer and recitation. Why? Because my father went to mosque and studied prayer and recitation, because my grandfather went to mosque and studied prayer and recitation, because my great-grandfather went to mosque and studied prayer and recitation. And I guess it kept going like that, stretching back from the father of my great-grandfather, to the grandfather of my great-grandfather, the great-grandfather of my great-grandfather, all the way back to Prophet Adam, from where there is no farther back to go. Apparently, all of them went to mosque and studied prayer recitation.

If I may be honest, I preferred going to watch the cock-fights behind the market, or going to the sports field to watch the pigeon races. That was way more exciting than sitting cross-legged in a prayer room, pronouncing letters I never used to recite, words whose meaning I didn't know. It was better to watch the horse dancers spin into trance at a party. Or argue over who'd won at cards. Or swim in the little stream that ran through the rice fields. Or watch the singers in an *orkes* band at a wedding. Or, in a big gang of kids, swarm a restaurant parking lot and wash the car windshields and force the drivers to give us some money for it. Or frisk a produce truck and steal a few juicy pieces of fruit.

But then I discovered grownups don't really like to see kids happy. So they start sending them to the mosque in the late afternoons. The army families sent their kids to the mosque. The village headman sent his kids to the mosque. The chicken porridge seller sent his kid to the mosque. The metalsmith sent his kid to the mosque. Even the town drunk sent his kid to the mosque. Every afternoon until night fell.

Really it wasn't all that bad, though. Kids always find a way to have fun. Long after I was grown, I'd still remember those times. We'd wear sarongs, more often slung over our shoulders than wrapped around our waist, and *peci* prayer hats a few sizes too big that slid around on our heads. I was happy because lots of my friends were there, and sometimes snacks were served. I'd see that bastard Asep and throw punches with Turman, and we'd all take turns singing into the mosque microphone. Its speaker would amplify our voices until they resounded over the whole settlement, before the pancake maker who had just had a baby would come hurrying over to twist our ears. Or before the village military liaison would come rip out the cord.

At that time, was I a pious child? Maybe, if you're basing it solely on the fact that I went to mosque every day. With the other children, I stood in the lines behind the grownups and prayed.

When it was time to say 'amen', we would compete to see who could say it the loudest and drag it out the longest, to make the limewash on the mosque ceiling come crumbling down and the cobwebs swing and sway from the beams. If I got the chance, I'd tug a friend's sarong so it fell off, or if he was standing in the line in front of me I could headbutt his ass, so he'd go crashing into the old folks in front of him, and so on, line after line, until half the congregation had collapsed on top of each other in a heap. If that happened, the kiai would be furious and interrupt the prayer. He'd come at us, ready to smack our butts with the huge wide palm of his hand, not caring who'd started the whole commotion, but my friends and I were always on the alert so we could go scrambling out of the mosque in all directions and escape. 'You dumb kids!' someone would swear—and that was fun too, we felt like the biggest rascals in the world. It wasn't anything complicated, but it really riled the old folks up. We'd be doubled over with laughter in the mosque yard, but still ready to run in case an adult was still aiming to grab us and yank on our ears.

One time, when we didn't dare go back to the mosque, we gathered on the side of the road. Kurnia, that stinky snot-nose, complained that his stomach was churning, but he didn't want to go back and use the mosque wash-room, afraid the kiai would ambush him, and he didn't want to go home and face his mother, because she'd yell that he hadn't gone to worship. We told him to go poop in a banana grove, so Kurnia found a plastic bag in a trash heap and disappeared into the shadows. It wasn't long before he re-emerged, the nasty snot-nose, the plastic bag filled with shit in his hand and a foul idea in his head.

He stood at the roadside with the bag dangling from his left hand. In the distance, the headlights of a city mini-bus could be seen slowly approaching. Kurnia waved his arm, signalling he wanted a ride. He was taller and stockier than most of the other kids, so he probably looked like an adult from far away and the bus slowed down and came to a stop right in front of him, thinking it had found a passenger. But instead of climbing aboard as the ticket-taker was expecting, Kurnia hurled the plastic bag inside. Sato Reang doesn't know whether the bag landed on an empty seat or a passenger's lap, but in all honesty, he hopes the contents splattered everywhere, because he's happy to imagine the world filled with all kinds of hilarious misfortune—it's ok to laugh at stuff like that.

Realizing what was in the bag, curses erupted from the driver, the ticket-taker, and all the passengers: 'You pig!'

'You dog!' 'You devil!'

'You're dead meat, dammit!'

The ticket-taker almost caught Kurnia, but this friend of ours was oh-so-nimble, he'd already leapt over the roadside ditch, and was racing back into the banana grove. The ticket-taker was fixing to give chase, but then he caught sight of all us other kids still gathered nearby, and it was like his eyes were shooting laser beams. Realizing the danger, especially since a few of the passengers were also starting to climb out, we followed suit and shot off, jumping over the little ditch after Kurnia, and vanished.

As we ran farther and farther, the calls and curses of the ticket-taker and the passengers faded into the distance. Gasping for breath, we found Kurnia behind the tofu factory. Now we were the ones cursing him, smacking his head from all sides.

'I swear on the devil's pubic hair, you're such an idiot!!'

Turman added, because he was the first to realize, 'And you didn't even wipe! You foul stinky dog!'

Kurnia just grinned wide, so wide. He said he'd wiped with a banana leaf. What an animal. Disgusting! Nasty! So dumb! Kurnia didn't care. He just kept smirking and smiling and scratching his butt. And after all, he wasn't the only one who sometimes had to poop in the grove and wipe with a banana leaf, so we soon forgot about it and thought up other ways to have fun that night, without having to go back to the mosque and without having to hurry home, because at such an hour once we'd gone inside it would be hard to get out again.

So back then, was Sato Reang a pious child? After considering everything I did in my childhood, the answer is, maybe not. At least not until I turned seven.

FATHER SAID IT WAS TIME FOR ME TO BE CIRCUMCISED. FINALLY! I thought. I knew what that meant, of course I did: the foreskin at the tip of my penis would be cut off. It would be snipped off with scissors, or chopped off with a machete, or sliced off with a knife.

Honestly at that time, and even for a while after, I didn't know exactly how a doctor cut off a boy's foreskin. Someone had told me that they used a heated sliver of hard bamboo. When I heard that, I got goosebumps over my entire body like my soul was slowly leaking away, but by the time I found out that Father was going to take me to a clinic during the school holiday, I had already kind of forgotten about it. Or if I did remember, I didn't care too much anymore because almost all of my friends had already gotten their foreskins cut off and they were totally fine. By then, and at that age, a peanut I'd accidentally got stuck up my nose was way more terrifying.

So I was feeling pretty chipper as I boasted to my friends and neighbours about the plan. I was hoping they would set aside some of their pocket money for me, because usually kids who were going to get circumcised would get cash and gifts from their family, friends, and neighbours. My uncle had already promised me a soccer jersey, Father had promised a bicycle, and my grandma was going to make me sweet coconut porridge. I swear, I had no idea that the day I lost my foreskin would be the day I stumbled into a trap, completely ignorant and unprepared.

'But why exactly does it have to be cut off?' asked a girl named Bunga, who lived just one house away.

Why? How should I know? Kids just did whatever the old folks told them to do, and *they* never seemed to want to explain anything. But to me, it was quite simple—obvious, really. A penis with its foreskin, in its natural form, was hideous. If you took a good look, it resembled a turtle head. Sometimes the head poked out and showed itself, sometimes it shrivelled up and vanished. It was weird. Ugly and gross. So of course part of it had to go, unless you wanted to carry a disgraceful turtle head around everywhere your whole life.

God forbid. It was unclean. I couldn't imagine my friends teasing, hey, there goes the turtle head guy! Just thinking about it made me shudder. Ugh.

So it was better just to cut it off. Learn from Amir, who'd had his removed last Ramadan, and Asep, whose thing looked way better without his. Cute. More polished. I liked it. Even though yes, it was true, if you looked closely, turns out now it resembled an eel snout. But that was okay. No one would insult me for it, because sooner or later all the boys would have their own.

The day arrived. Before dawn I stood there between Father and Uncle, waiting for a city minibus. The doctor's clinic was a bit far away, a half an hour trip, and we had to get there very early in the morning because during a school vacation like this, there would be lots of boys with the very same plan.

Thankfully we got an empty minibus, with only one other passenger. In the mornings, the ones going from the market toward the outskirts were always quiet—they'd get crowded once they were headed back in the other direction.

At the clinic, the doctor told me to lie down on a high, narrow cot. A young nurse was assisting him, getting everything ready. She folded a sarong and placed it on my chest, probably so I wouldn't be able to see what the doctor was doing down by my legs. Now that's smart, I thought. When it was all over I could take the sarong home as a gift.

But then I felt my body go a little cold. I couldn't help it, I was starting to get nervous. What if the doctor cut it wrong? What if he cut off my dick, the entire thing? Ah, I thought, son of a bitch. That better not happen. How would I pee? Maybe I should start to scream, beg Father not to be circumcised after all—was it absolutely necessary? But that thought quickly evaporated, as soon as I imagined my friends' taunts and teases—back then I didn't know that infidels weren't circumcised and they felt just fine with a turtle head in their pants. Gathering my courage, I said to myself: I will get through this. It'll only take a moment. It won't hurt. Or at least it won't hurt worse than getting bitten by a red ant.

Two plus four equals six. Six plus nine equals fifteen. The capital of North Korea is Pyongyang. Albert Einstein invented the lightbulb. Aw, dang, I knew that one was wrong.

'What's your name?' the young nurse asked. A little startled, I looked over at her. Dammit, she could tell I was nervous. With her question, with her smile, with her kind expression, she was trying to calm me down. I felt a little insulted. I didn't need to be bucked up, I didn't need any comforting. I was just getting circumcised, there was no need to make such a big deal about it. In this world some people had lost an arm, or a leg, or an eye, and they were still treated with dignity and respect! I hated the way she was looking at me, as if she saw herself as some protective older sister who was ready to hug me and shield me from misfortune.

Even so, I answered her question. 'Sato Reang.'

'It's over,' she said.

What was over? Was our conversation over? Or was the world over–had it come to an end, was it doomsday? Then I understood, the procedure was over. The doctor had already cut off my foreskin, and I hadn't even realized that he'd started or seen how he'd done it. I felt nothing, and for a second I wondered whether it was all just a trick. To reassure me the young nurse peered at my bottom half to take a closer look. I felt embarrassed. I wanted to scream, Hey what are you looking at! Get out of there! Have you no decency, woman, just looking down at someone's thing, ogling me like that!

'It's a very small wound. You're a sweet child, I hope you heal up quickly.' Sweet child, she said.

I felt the skin of my cheeks tightening, and if anyone had been paying attention they might have seen them flush red. I was holding my tongue but I really wanted to snap at her: 'I don't like being called a sweet child, I'd much prefer you call me a baby monkey!' But right at that moment I felt a small tingling in my penis. So it was true, the doctor had done his job.

Luckily, the young nurse stepped aside. She began straightening up the equipment and I didn't even have the chance to see whether he'd used a pair of scissors, a knife, or a sliver of hard bamboo. The doctor looked over to Father and Uncle, who had been waiting this whole time on a long bench at one side of the room. You can come take a look if you'd like, the doctor said, and in unison Father and Uncle stood up and approached me.

Father stood on my right, Uncle walked around to my left. Even then I couldn't tell that something big was about to happen, that my fate was about to be sealed—but all the years that followed, everything that would come to pass, started on that day. I looked up at my uncle, then at my father. They looked somewhat alike, though Uncle was a little thinner, his face more tapered.

'Today, your foreskin has been cut,' Father said.

Everyone in the room already knew that, but of course adults love to talk and talk, and their lives are like the words that come out of their mouths, a drawn-out waste of time. But then I realized that although his words had no meaning by themselves, they were the prelude to a kind of deal. A kind of contract he would force me into—and I didn't have to nod, didn't have to shake hands, I didn't even have to consent or agree.

Something was coming. I waited.

'And now it is time for you to become a pious child.'

A PIOUS CHILD, HE SAID. BEFORE I'D GONE TO SCHOOL, I'D OFTEN thought that once I was grown, I'd join the forest police, mostly because of the forest policeman who passed by our house every few days on his way to work. But instead I was being told to become a pious child! This damn father of mine, why didn't he want me to become some other kind of person? At least he could have said, 'And now it is time for you to become a well digger,' because I'd also been obsessed with well diggers and hoped to maybe become one someday.

Ah, but what did any of that matter anymore. Father had told me what I would be. Sato Reang. Must. Become. A Pious. Child.

Ooof. I really didn't want to! Oh heck. A year before there had been a boy who was two years older than me, and he was not cool or interesting or fun in any way. Any time you invited him to play, he didn't want to and his reason was always this: 'I'm afraid to sin.' Steal a mango, he was afraid to sin. Bet on cards, afraid to sin. Borrow a girl's clothes and pretend to be a woman, he'd call you a friend of Satan. It was rough. Like really grim. Luckily he and his parents had moved away, I don't know where to, but we all were thankful.

Aside from that, becoming a pious child meant I would have to pray five times a day. Recite the Qu'ran in Arabic at night. I couldn't eat or drink from dawn till dusk during the fasting month. I had to fear God and if I wanted something, I'd have to ask Him for it. Why couldn't kids just laze around? Go running in dried out ditches chasing lizards? In my heart, I vowed to disobey.

But because it seemed like becoming a forest policeman or a well digger would take forever, in the days that followed I just tried to do whatever I could—above all, whatever made me happy. Catching butterflies and peeling off their wings, for example, was really fun, even though Bunga would punch me in the head with her fist if she caught me doing it, calling me a savage, and I didn't dare hit her back because she was a girl and because she had an older brother who was already huge. That dumb-bell. To get back at her, I stomped on an anthill with my sandal, even though she didn't know I did it.

A few days later I forgot about that, just like I'd forgotten about catching butterflies. The farm kids from the village near the forest went crazy over crickets. Our city was small, people called it Stone Swamp, and the kids that lived near the center of town, not far from the market and the town square, wanted to join in the fun. That's how my playmates and I started trying to capture crickets. We roamed the fields that were being left to dry out, dug along the large cracks in the earth, lifted stones, and lunged after the leaping bugs. A few times we caught some beetles but not many of us succeeded in catching any crickets, so we ended up just buying a few from the farm kids, along with some cages to keep them in. Every afternoon, we'd gather on a patch of empty land, squat back on our haunches, and fight those crickets.

I'd starve mine the whole day, believing that was the way to win, just as the farm kids who'd sold them to me taught me to. A few friends would leave their cages next to cages full of female crickets the night before. Others fed theirs chili peppers.

All of these tricks were said to make them fierce. When a cricket was put in a hollow of dirt with another cricket, they would attack each other. Collide. Pinch. Bite. Shove. One of the crickets might lose a leg, or its antenna would get ripped off, and its owner would halt the match, admit defeat. Once we left a cricket in the ring until it died, its head ripped off and sent rolling.

'Mampus!'

That meant it was dead meat. I always loved hearing someone yell out that word. It was like fire was coming out of his mouth, erupting like hot smoke.

I wanted to know how it felt. I squatted, watching my cricket, who was fighting for its life against Turman's cricket. Charge! Attack! Chomp! Chew!

All these words thundered in my head, but nothing came out of my mouth. My cricket moved unpredictably—he rammed into his opponent, but then retreated in a circle. Then they faced each other again, jaws moving. I wanted to bang the dry earth where we'd gathered, so that those crickets would be more ferocious, and never lose their nerve to kill or be killed.

I crouched there, all riled up, my hair prickling with sweat under the scorching afternoon sun. But suddenly the atmosphere went quiet. I looked up at my friends. They were looking back at me with concern, but they didn't say a word. They knew something I didn't. Danger, I thought.

But when I looked over my shoulder, it was Father, towering over me like a beefy giant, even though in retrospect I now know he was only a little over five feet tall.

We stared at each other under the boiling sun. 'Go to the mosque,' he said. Short and curt.

I longed to rake up a handful of the dry earth and throw it in his face, smother him with the reddish sand. Grownups don't know their place, I thought, showing up just to embarrass their own kid in front of all his friends. They think they're so big. So powerful. Just because he was the one who fed and clothed me—so what? I looked toward my friends, hoping they would take my side, but damn! All I saw was fear on their faces. Not just that—quietly they were all scooping up their crickets, live and dead, putting them into their cages and slowly, one by one, they were retreating.

I understood. They didn't want to risk it. Every kid knew that grownups could be cruel. Grownups might suddenly snatch up those cricket cages and destroy them. In one fell swoop, grownups might hit, slap, yank, pinch. It was better not to get involved with them. Run. Keep your distance. Save yourself. That's what my friends were doing. In the distance they stood behind tree trunks, or looked out at me from between the bushes, waiting—far enough away to run if threatened, but close enough to return to the cricket fighting arena if they had the opportunity.

Those monkeys!

'Go to the mosque!' I heard my father's voice again, louder this time, and harsh.

I looked back at my friends. They were no longer waiting. One by one they were disappearing, maybe looking for a new spot. Now it was just Father and me.

I had to accept my fate. With dragging steps, I followed after Father. I couldn't refuse, my head bowed as if there was a rope with one end in Father's hand and the other tied around my neck, like a herdsman dragging his buffalo.

In the distance, the call to prayer sounded faintly from the mosque tower.

And maybe that was the moment that I truly felt how deeply—how utterly and completely—I did not want to become a pious child. And that feeling just kept growing and growing.

I STARTED TO TRULY ADMIRE KIDS WHO NEVER WENT TO THE MOSQUE, wondering how they and their parents could be freed from the contract of making pious children. Around the neighbourhood, and in school, there were a few kids like that. They ruled the world, I thought—or at least, they enjoyed it more than I could. And it was then that I started to wonder whether somewhere on this earth there were boys whose foreskins weren't cut, although I only got my answer many years later.

Father didn't completely forbid me from enjoying life. Like other kids, I made kites and went to the outskirts of the village to fly them on dry fields. When the seasons changed and those fields were flooded, I hunted for eels there, amidst the wet rice paddies, or beetles. Other times, we walked side by side down to the bay on mornings when there was no school, and swam there, returning home carrying a bunch of fish after helping some fishermen pull in their nets. Even so, especially at dusk, if I hadn't come home and it was getting near time to pray, Father would come looking for me, just as he had when I was cricket-fighting.

That had truly made me ashamed—beyond ashamed, I felt denigrated. I'm serious. Little kids can feel such things, and I carried that piercing pain well into adulthood, long after my beard and mustache grew. How I'd been forced to put my crickets back in their cage, stand up, and follow Father home. How I'd clutched the cage tight to my chest, trying not to cry, my vision blurring but no tears falling.

Out of all the other kids I wished I could trade places with, Tongos was the one I admired most of all. My mother had a kiosk at the market, and so on my way home from school, I would often stop by to do some shopping and get lunch, and I would see him wandering around. Tongos wasn't that much older than me, but he didn't go to school. He wasn't ever bothered by the call to prayer that came five times a day. No one forced him to go shower or change his shirt, which I could see growing shabby from days of wear. I heard his father and mother lived in a hut with his uncle. Out of all of them only Tongos could talk, and appeared to be the most sound of mind. His father, mother, and uncle were a little bit crazy, or at least that's what people said.

One afternoon I saw some people grabbing Tongos. They slapped him on his left cheek and right cheek. The loud *plak, plak* made me shiver, made my own skin seem to sting. At first I felt sorry for Tongos, especially since it was grownups hitting him, three men and one woman who also twisted his ear and pulled up on it so that Tongos had to go up on his tiptoes. I was overcome with pity and amazement. The feeling still haunts my soul to this day.

'Devil child! You think you can steal?!'

Tongos didn't scream, didn't moan, didn't beg them to stop their torture. I admired his ability to withstand suffering, but it wasn't just that—I was amazed that he could drive those people so crazy, just beside themselves with anger—to make them feel so threatened and so upset. And Tongos responded to all their insults, saying simply, 'Hungry! I was hungry!'

I realized what the issue was. He had stolen something, maybe money, maybe food. But it was beyond obvious that he was starving. His family often went hungry, and if they couldn't scavenge anything from the trash to eat or sell, they would beg. Tongos didn't seem to feel ashamed, and he seemed to have lost all trace of fear. He had stolen, he'd been caught stealing, and he would certainly steal again.

I went home, lay down on my bed, and let my thoughts drift and float. I imagined myself stealing and getting caught.

People would recognize me right away. Someone would say, 'Oh, that's Umar's boy.'

I wouldn't cry. Even if they twisted my ear or slapped my face, I wouldn't beg for mercy.

And if they brought me to the police station, I would walk in with my head held high. How wonderful that would be. How wonderful to humiliate Father.

Sato Reang had become a purple plastic ball. He'd brought the ball to the prayer house yard. He'd invited Bandi and a pair of brothers, Sofyan and Mahfud to play a match, two against two. The four boys took off their flip-flops and used them as goal markers, two pairs on each side of the field. They let their bare feet tread on the damp earth, kicking up mud here, dust there, trampling grass, stomping on pebbles. Sato Reang was the oldest of the group; it was a few months after his visit to the circumcision clinic.

The prayer house yard was shaded by great big sapodilla trees. It was spacious and the dirt was swept flat and even. As they ran, taking turns dribbling the ball, their feet started to turn red—the ball's surface wasn't smooth, there were raised lines that curved around it, making pentagons and hexagons, and there was a seam around its middle with sharp bits of plastic sticking out. Small welts appeared on their skin where they'd been smacked and nicked, but they didn't care. They whooped, they yelled, they laughed out loud. Sweating, panting, covered in dirt.

Even then I'd started to think, in the simplest way, that as a child my life was no better than a soccer ball's. It went rolling along because someone kicked it, and if it was kicked hard it would advance quickly, whizzing through the air, twisting and turning a bit as the breeze teased it along. If someone picked the ball up and held it, though, it couldn't budge.

It's possible the life of a ball, even a cheap plastic one, is interesting. People are cheered by its presence, after all, and in a wide open field, it can become the center of attention—but it's still just a ball. And that's what I felt like as a child. They dragged me. They pushed me. They talked at me, and forced me to listen to what they said. You must go to school. Must go to mosque. Must recite verses, must memorize prayers. Must finish your rice. Mustn't forget to brush your teeth.

The world I lived in was like a never-ending nag. To those who say childhood is a happy time, I can only snort. They can't know anything about it—it's as if they'd arrived on earth with a head full of grey hair and a beard like some kind of billy goat.

Afternoon was starting to slide into night. A handful of old men, who made up the tiny congregation, could be spotted in the distance, slowly shuffling toward the prayer house from different directions. Then Kiai Jumadi also appeared. He had built the prayer house on his own land, without seeking a permit or any kind of permission. According to him, a house of God could stand anywhere. Originally he'd intended it just for himself and for his family to use, but a few neighbours, who suffered from rheumatism and gout and strokes, whose bum legs were sore and whose joints ached, whose toes were stiff and couldn't walk a long way, started to join him there.

Now Kiai Jumadi saw the four boys playing soccer and approached them, lifting up a corner of his sarong.

'Game's over! Break it up! Time to pray!'

None of them listened. They just kept running and jostling over the ball.

'Break it up! I said: Break it up! Didn't you hear me?!'

Sato Reang had heard, but he'd decided to pretend he hadn't. Playing soccer was much more fun than praying, and lately he'd begun to get the feeling that he himself could choose what he wanted to do. He didn't want to pray. He didn't want to be a pious child. He wanted to chase the ball—dodging, kicking, knocking shins with Sofyan.

Night had now truly fallen. The yard had grown dim. But as long as the four boys could make each other out in the weak yellowish glow from the lamp hung from the prayer house roof, as long as they could follow the ball, they felt no need to stop—and especially not Bandi and Sofyan, who were losing to Sato Reang and Mahfud, 0-2.

'Don't try to cheat,' Bandi said, 'and don't even think of quitting now. I can still beat you guys.'

Sato Reang happily obliged.

Not far from their village, there was a real soccer field, owned by the military. But dammit, the guys never let them play. They were always forced to be onion boys, warming the bench, only allowed on the field if the big kids were short on players. Now, with their own ball, and the large mosque yard to themselves, they felt like they had the right to play to their heart's content.

Bats flapped among the trees. This was the sign of day turning to night, or the reverse. They moved so quickly through the air, like shadows, but left the sense of friction, a rustling of leaves.

I would often mark time with things like that, to provide a kind of boundary between the past, the moment I was living in, and the time yet to come. The past was over, boring. The future was thrilling, mysterious, and I often contemplated it—but more than anything, I wanted to be the master of my own present, because I was right smack in the middle of it. It was the absolute best if I was steering the ship, but it could turn into something wretched if I couldn't do what I wanted, if my present was held in someone else's grip.

Resenting the bigger kids' control of the military field, Sato Reang had sworn he'd buy his own ball. He'd seen one hanging in front of a small shop, in a large basket with all the others. Sato Reang had saved up some pocket money—his mother would often send him running to the corner store to buy soap, flour, or sugar, and he got to keep the change—and he'd brought that ball home. He played with it in front of his house, kicking it against two banana trees. The next day he tried to play against some chickens. He passed to them, but they were so stupid, instead of stopping the ball with their fat bodies, they would hop into the air, flapping their wings: it was as if, as members of the bird family, some ancient wisdom was still echoing in their little brains that they should be able to fly.

Sato Reang began to feel like the ball was his friend.

Then family. They grew to be inseparable. Wherever he ran, the ball rolled after. He felt himself soar every time the ball was kicked into the sky. But only in retrospect did he realize that he *was* the ball. The ball *was* him. To be a child was to be nothing more than a ball.

Members of Kiai Jumadi's congregation began to arrive. As one hobbled by, hunched over his cane on the way into the small mosque, he chided, 'Better watch out! If you keep playing out here in the dark, a demon will possess you!' Of course the boys didn't care about demons. They'd never seen one, nor someone possessed by one. They'd only seen soccer.

2-1. Sofyan sent the ball rolling through two piles of sandals. No one was thinking about Satan, but if he did actually exist, he would have been happy that they kept playing when they should have been praying. Their shirts were sticky with sweat.

The old men just rubbed their chests in consternation, realizing their appeals were being carried away with the wind. They went in, surrendering the boys' fate to the creeping darkness.

KIAI JUMADI HELD HIS HAND UP TO HIS MOUTH AND CHANTED THE call to prayer. His voice was quickly drowned out by a much louder call, coming from the speaker set atop the Sowing the Seeds of Our Heavenly Land Mosque. This mosque stood at the opposite edge of the settlement, but its call to prayer travelled, colliding with the same calls coming from a few other mosques in the area. No one knew why every mosque tried to be the loudest, the shrillest, but one thing was clear—the cacophony in the air didn't distract those kids. The plastic ball kept rolling, moving from one foot to another, getting dribbled and passed, then sent aloft.

Bandi's foot was bleeding a little bit. It had been scraped by a shard of plastic as he was trying to steal the ball from Mahfud. He grimaced.

'Should we stop?' Sato Reang asked in sympathy.

'No,' said Bandi.

The last glow of twilight had disappeared. Stars were appearing in the sky. Sato Reang took another look at Bandi's small injury, then nodded in agreement. Going home could only mean one thing: his mother would tell him to hurry to Sowing the Seeds of Our Heavenly Land Mosque to catch up with his father.

Kiai Jumadi had begun to lead the prayer, with the eight stooped old folks lined up neatly behind him, except for the one who'd had a stroke and prayed sitting down.

But they didn't just pray. Usually at night, between the dusk and Isha prayers, they also recited the Qur'an. Chanting synchronous praise to the Prophet. Begging for God's mercy, also synchronized, and in between these prayers slipping in the hope that God would forever open the hearts of children—all children, including the four still running wild and oblivious in the mosque yard. The worshippers were tied to one another by their age, by their decline, by their ever depleting will to live, which was being gradually replaced by their collective submission to an ever-diminishing future.

This prayer house didn't have a microphone, and when Kiai Jumadi read the prayers his voice was so soft it was almost inaudible. So were the voices of those behind him, as if their sighed amens were meant only for each other's ears.

But at the end of the second 'Amen,' they were startled by a deafening crash. *Duarrr*! Their weakening hearts seized up simultaneously, almost stopped dead, their souls collectively made to leap right out of their frail bodies once and for all.

The shock almost toppled Kiai Jumadi right over. For a few moments he could not continue—his lips trembled, his hands shook, and his legs wobbled as, with all their might, they tried to hold the burden of his body up. When he could speak again, instead of returning to the reading he began, without even realizing it, a murmured entreaty, 'I take refuge in the Lord from the temptations of the Devil.'

But it was just those kids in the yard. Bandi had aimed for a goal to tie the score, and the ball just barely missed. Sato Reang moved fast, he ran, and at the exactly right moment, he swooped in and aimed at the ball with his right foot, a powerful kick, the plastic ball went flying, and, whizzing, it slammed right into the window shutters, making the walls of woven bamboo shudder and the cobwebs swing violently in the corners—and came close to accidentally murdering every old man inside.

It was a very simple prayer house. The floor was cement, a few feet off the ground (so that they'd had to build a small stoop leading up to the terrace), and covered in black tile, which kept things cool in the daytime but felt freezing cold at night. To warm it up, the front half of the floor was covered with woven pallets and pandan leaves. Those coming to pray brought their own prayer mats for extra cushioning.

The posts were made from coconut tree trunks. The lower half of the walls were made from cement and bricks, and the upper half, which were made of woven bamboo, had already been replaced twice. A swarm of wasps had made their nest on one corner of the roof. In another corner, there was a small cupboard storing a few folded sarongs and some musty old prayer mats. A few copies of the Qur'an were lying on one of the shelves, their covers falling off, their pages ripped.

The atmosphere settled back into stillness. The nine old men were once again absorbed in their silent prayer recitation. Only their right index fingers moved occasionally, lifting up off their knees slightly to indicate that there is only one God. The only sounds came from the four boys outside. Screaming. Teasing. Whooping. Laughing.

When his prayers were done, Kiai Jumadi came out of the prayer house, approaching the boys and fixing to snatch up the plastic ball but with their childish agility they easily kept it away from him. Kiai Jumadi also tried to whack the ball with his cane, but at first he couldn't make contact and then one of the swings actually sent the ball flying straight up, almost striking him, just a hair from his forehead. The colour drained from his face and he once again mumbled for God's protection from these uncivilized little devils, thinking that he should report the kids to their parents, hoping that a long switch would whip their legs in punishment.

While he was silently grumbling, one of the kids called out, chuckling, 'Sorry, Kiai. It was an accident.'

Another said, 'Kiai, just go back into the prayer house.'

'You cursed willful children!' the Kiai muttered furiously, but immediately regretted his emotion. The devil is tempting me, he thought. He returned to quiet, penitent whispers for God's protection. He had no other choice—he didn't have the energy to yell at them or strike them himself. He could no longer catch up with kids like that. He turned around and went back into the prayer house.

To remember God. To read the Qur'an, portion by portion. Who knows how many times over the course of his life he'd read that holy book, from the first verse to the last, before reciting the whole thing again, and over and over like that, on and on and on.

I saw the Kiai go back into the surau. He paid us no more attention. The prayer house enveloped him, and he returned to seeking peace.

OLD FOLKS HAVE FEARS ABOUT NIGHT FALLING, WHICH I'VE NEVER understood. They see it as a time of danger and threat, as if the creeping chill in the air is the harbinger of all kinds of sickness. My mother would almost always call me inside, telling me to come quickly because it was dusk. When night fell everything had to stop—only one thing could go on: prayer.

Suddenly I wondered, is mother looking for me? Who knows. Mother tended to assume the best. When she hadn't seen me playing ball with the chickens and the coconut trees in our yard, she must have thought I'd gone straight to the mosque.

It was also quite likely she didn't realize I hadn't bathed yet. If she had known I was still splattered with mud, and wasn't at the mosque, she would have gone out with a flashlight, hunting all around, questioning our neighbours. At that time my sister hadn't been born yet, I was her one and only child. It was only because she thought I had gone with Father that she wasn't worried.

We kept playing. Bandi and Sofyan kept trying to kick the ball into my goal.

Someone must have seen us, and that was the start of the whole catastrophe. Someone had walked by, but we never found out who—maybe someone coming home from the mosque, or some office worker getting home late, who knows, but he must have been walking along the footpath that cut through the groves that grew by the prayer house and, hidden in the shadows of the sapodilla trees, he probably stopped to look at us. I only caught a glimpse of his shadow. He left without a word and none of us really paid him any attention.

But not long after that, Sato Reang saw his father appear. He was still wearing a black *peci* prayer hat and his sarong was still wrapped around his waist. Clearly, after prayers at the Sowing the Seeds of Our Heavenly Land Mosque, he had stopped by the house for a moment to get a machete from the kitchen. Sato Reang recognized it immediately—Father often used it to hack dried leaves off the banana trees in the small garden behind the house. Now it was swinging in his right hand, unsheathed. As he appeared, the rays of lamplight coming down from the roof reflected off its large, flat blade.

Bandi saw him too. So did Sofyan and Mahfud. Without giving another thought to the score, which was still 2-1, wasting no time at all, the three boys quickly snatched up their flip-flops and their small feet hurried away, vanishing through the bushes at the edge of the mosque yard. Running silently. Saving themselves. Don't get involved with an angry grownup, especially not if he's holding a machete. Every kid understands that simple rule.

The ball rolled to a stop right in front of his father. Though he wanted to flee like his friends, Sato Reang didn't budge—he couldn't get his legs to work and besides, where could he really go? The only place he could think to run to was his own house, and his father would obviously find him there.

His father didn't say even one word. He stooped over to pick up the ball and then he squatted down, shoving it firmly down into the dirt. He didn't look at Sato Reang, his eyes were focused murderously on the ball. Making sure the boy could see him, he punctured the ball, then slid the blade into the slit. When the blade sawed against the ball's thick plastic, out came a loud *nyit-nyit-nyit.*

The sound made Sato Reang's head throb. The hair on the back of his neck stood up. He felt that plastic ball was him, and the machete was cutting his body in half—impaling him, splitting him through to the very core of his being.

Leaving the ball splayed apart in the dirt, like two empty bowls facing the sky, Father turned around and went home without a word. Ever since then, Sato Reang had felt like he was a plastic ball that had been split in two. That pain never let up, what with his soul pierced through, leaking out, left in pieces, gaping and exposed.

He heard that sound every time he passed by a shop that had a big basket filled with plastic balls hanging out front. He heard it every time he saw another kid playing ball. He even heard it whenever he saw anything round or anything purple.

His body felt split apart every time he heard the call to prayer resounding from the mosque rooftop speaker. A pain travelling like a current from the crown of his head right down between his legs, every time he saw a modest prayer house or a grand mosque.

His father and his machete and that purple plastic ball were never far from his thoughts. As his father walked away with the machete still in hand, leaving the ball cleaved in two, Sato Reang still didn't move from where he stood. He just watched his father's back grow smaller, his legs carrying him further away.

After a few moments, his feet began to move. He never touched that ball again, he just left its remnants splayed open in the mosque yard. He walked away from it, heading for home. He never knew what became of its two halves. Did Kiai Jumadi take them? Did Bandi, Sofyan, or Mahfud come back in secret to find them there, and even though they knew it could no longer be used, did they bring the wreckage home? Or did the plastic ball lie there all night, with no one touching it, until some trash collector passed by and scooped it into his sack?

Back at home, his father was waiting. Sato decided not to be afraid, not to shrink back. Though it had occurred to him to run away he would accept his fate, just like the ball, whatever that fate might be. He didn't see the machete, maybe it was already back in the small wooden cabinet in the storage shed. His father was holding Sato's sarong, and when he saw his son, he hurled it at him.

'Go pray. Right now!'

Sato Reang decided not to speak. He picked up the sarong, went to the washroom to do his ablutions, and then entered the small prayer room. Looking back on it years later, those had been the longest prayers of his life. Because he recited them a few times slower than usual.

With that day, his childhood was over. There were no more afternoons spent kicking the plastic ball around with his friends, no more cricket-fighting until they bit the dust. There were no more dark nights where a friend hailed a city minibus and threw a bag full of shit inside.

IN THE EVENINGS AFTER PRAYER I ALSO STUDIED RECITATION. I HAD been doing it at the mosque but because I used to goof off with the other kids and my ability to read Arabic never seemed to improve, Father told me to study at home. I had made my way through the short verses, and now I had to read the Qur'an starting from the first surat.

What can I say, I guess my tongue wasn't so good at pronouncing the words. Plus, I'd never even met any Arabs or heard them speak their language, so I truly didn't know how they were supposed to sound, exactly. I just tried to imitate whatever Father wanted me to sound like, but I was always just waiting for that inevitable moment when he would yell, 'Wrong!'

And my mistakes always seemed to repeat themselves. If one day I could remember a word correctly, the next day on a different page I would forget and make the same error. Father usually sat listening on our shabby sofa, which was so broken down that when he sat there it looked no different from squatting. He would be smoking, but he was listening intently. Again and again he would yell 'Wrong!' or 'Start over!'

When I made too many mistakes, I would hear him start to breathe heavily. Maybe he was holding back curses. I had once seen my friend's father get mad at him and yell, 'You pig, where are your brains? Use your brains! Listen! Perk up your ears, scour out all that wax. You little piglet. Yeah, cry! Go ahead, cry! What's the point of living if you're this stupid!' But no, Father never indulged in such things. When he was irritated he grew quiet, only his breath seemed to seethe. Still, that was enough to turn my palms cold. And the back of my neck. I didn't dare glance his way, let alone catch his eye.

'Do it again!'

I repeated the last line, my thoughts flying far far away. For the first time, Sato Reang began to think: what if Father didn't exist?What if there were no mosque? What if he didn't need to pray?

What if he didn't need to have his foreskin cut off, because he didn't need to be a pious child.

THE DREAM FIRST CAME TO HIM WHEN HE WAS TWELVE, AND IT would often return at unexpected times. In that dream he was in a small skiff, all alone, in the middle of the ocean. Wherever he looked, he could see nothing but the horizon, a huge circle around him. There were no islands, no ships. There were no large waves, nothing disturbed the surface of the water except a few small ripples gently rocking his boat. He was holding an oar, and was slowly paddling.

It seemed peaceful, but the dream left him with a feeling of impending, overwhelming dread. The ocean revealed nothing, a perpetual mystery, but what if something sucked his boat down into the depths? What if a sea monster appeared before him, a kind he'd never even heard of, and ferociously attacked? What if the boat carried him into a whirlpool? What if he never saw anything or anyone ever again, and spent the rest of his life in loneliness and silence?

Would he find a place to land, or would he be drifting in uncertainty forever? In his dream, even the rippling water made no sound.

Dokkk-dokkk! *Dokkk-dokkk*! His father is banging on his door. It's four in the morning, he's never late.

The pounding assails his ears, and Sato Reang tries to get up, but he can't. His eyelids feel too heavy to open, his head is sunken down into the pillow, his back glued to the mattress. He tries to roll his body over onto its side but it's too heavy.

His pillows and mattress are made of thick cotton batting. It's not exactly hard, but it's not soft either. Every few weeks, Mother tells him to drag it out into the sun, so it won't get damp and mouldy. It takes two or more people to lug it out into the yard, and spread it out flat atop a row of wooden planks. Under the hot sun, he beats it with a rattan stick, every blow sending a poof of fine dust flying, like a white mist. The sun warms it and chases out all the little bugs nesting in its folds.

The dream didn't just give him an anxious feeling that danger was lurking, it also gave him a strange pleasure. Nudging and nuzzling, that feeling was also there, in his heart, poking out, as if asking him to get acquainted.

Long after, I realized that that happiness came from the wide expanse of the ocean, from the feeling that I could go wherever I wanted, not caring that I had no destination, nothing to move toward. I paddled as hard as I could. Nothing was tethering the boat and no one was blocking its way. The ocean was a vast expanse, and it was all mine. I could explore every bit of it, for the rest of my life. I could move fast, or slow, whatever I felt like, it was all up to me. I could hoot and holler without bothering anyone, just as I could sing without following a tune. *Aeooo, aeooo...*

Is there anything more joyful than for a fish to swim free in the sea, even if danger might be lurking? Wouldn't people be happy living without the burdens of having to do this or that? Having to bow down to The Great Creator and do good unto others? In the sea, alone, I didn't need to worry about all that. *Aeooo, aeooo...*

Dokkk-dokkk! *Dokkk-dokkk*! *Dokkk-dokkk*! Now Father's pounding on the door sounded louder. He was doing it with the knuckles of his clenched fist. His father would never leave, would never stop until he was sure the boy was awake. Now he called out, 'Get up, Sato! Get up! Time to pray!'

Prayers weren't something they could ignore. If they were sleeping, they had to get up. If they were working, they had to stop. If they were on a journey, they would pray along the way. Even if they were sick, they still had to pray—they'd be praying on their deathbed. Father had hammered that into Sato Reang's head, ever since he'd had his foreskin cut off, and it had been hammered in by his prayer recitation teachers, and after that by the preacher, and so Father didn't have to say anything else, just call him and bang on the door.

His father tended to wake up quite early. Usually he fell asleep just before midnight, and then only briefly. After a few hours he was awake again but, trying not to awaken anyone else, including his wife and his daughter who was now part of their family, he would go to the washroom to splash water on his face, do his ablutions, and then say his Isha prayers.

Their house had a small prayer room, and there he would

spend some time, in almost complete silence, with only the faint sounds of a passing car in the distance mingling with the equally faint crashing of waves on the beach. Or the humming of the insects in the trees in their yard, the occasional chirping of a bird.

But that peace would end when his knuckles pounded on his son's bedroom door.

THERE WAS A MAGAZINE KIOSK AT THE FAR END OF THE MARKET, near the bus terminal. They sold all kinds of magazines, newspapers, and pocket paperbacks. Once a week Sato Reang went there to buy a small magazine with a simple name, *Crosswords*. More than half of its 64 pages were filled with puzzles; there were a few ads on the cover and a few back pages providing the solutions to the previous edition's puzzles, and listing the names of quiz winners—anyone could enter by sending their answers with the coupon printed on the very last page, and you could win a motorbike, a television, a rice cooker, and cash.

He can't remember when he started to enjoy crossword puzzles. But what other choices did he have to entertain himself? If he bought something and brought it home, and his father looked over and said 'what's that?' crosswords were the only thing that would elicit nothing more than a short nod. His father let him be, so those magazines were piled up on the desk in his room. They were officially released every Wednesday, but he could get the new edition at the kiosk late Tuesday afternoon on his way home from school. Then at night, after finishing his homework, he could sit at his desk and start to fill in the first page.

That page was the easiest, he did it in under ten minutes and moved on to the second page. But now he started to stumble—he couldn't get one across or two down, even with some letters filled in. Sato Reang opened a popular encyclopaedia. It had been his father's, and he'd taken it to help with the crosswords, but this time it was no help at all. He opened the dictionary, checked the small notebook where he recorded new vocabulary, still no answer.

He'd planned to go to sleep after the second puzzle, but now he was fixated, trying all different letters in the empty boxes, scribbling on scrap paper, coming up with bizarre and likely non-existent words. He started thinking maybe they'd given the wrong clue, though that had never happened before, and still not quite ready to go to sleep, Sato Reang decided to do the puzzle on the third page. It wasn't as easy as the first, but he could fill it all in with the help of the encyclopaedia, dictionary, and his notebook. And so he turned back to the second page, determined.

Suddenly he realized the alarm clock on his desk showed it was after midnight. He quickly shut the magazine, climbed into bed, lay down, and pulled up his blanket. His mouth opened in a wide yawn. His head was growing heavy. His body was flying, his soul was just descending into the depths of sleep when he heard the old '*Dokkk-dokkk*! *Dokkk-dokkk*!' It was faint and far away, but still a little startling.

By the second knock, Sato Reang was thoroughly awake. The pounding tormented his ears, he felt like the curtain of his sleep was being ripped off, torn to shreds. It was still hard to get his body to move, but he felt something pulling it by force.

Let me sleep just for one or two more hours, he silently pleaded, not sure to whom.

Dokkk-dokkk! *Dokkk-dokkk*! Five or ten minutes later. 'Sato! Get up now! It's time for Subuh prayer!'

He heard his father's deep voice and he knew it would never stop. Soon, if there was no sign that his son was up and responding, his father would open the door. There was only one way to prevent his father from entering and yanking on his legs, pulling him from sleep.

'I'm coming!' Sato Reang yelled.

Reluctantly, I sat up and swung my legs over the side of the bed, letting them dangle there for a minute. My spirit was still in the realm of dreams, and I was trying to call it, to drag it back into my body. Why couldn't I sleep late like Topan? He could get up just five minutes before the school bell rang and make it on time. He managed a quick wash and even breakfast. Why couldn't I be like that?

Why couldn't I be like Ridwan, his parents never bugged him about going to mosque, never pestered him to pray. And he was still a good kid. He shared his snacks, when he had pocket money to buy them. Nothing foul ever came out of his mouth. The girls liked him because he treated them well, and listened to their chatter without interrupting. I was sure that Ridwan would grow up to be a respectable person—maybe a ship captain, or maybe he would move to a big city and open a jewellery store, or go travelling and study abroad, all without ever having had to wake up early in the morning.

I thought about all this while sitting on the side of my bed, my head swinging and swaying it was so heavy. Why...

'Now!'

'Yes.'

His father left the house and Sato Reang followed a few steps behind. The sky was still practically pitch black all around him, the damp air frigid, not a single cock crowing, no birds chirping at one another from the branches. No hint of the sun visible in the east, only some mice skittering out of someone's kitchen and stars hanging in a clear sky.

Sato Reang walked, but felt like he was floating—his head empty but also teetering, about to fall. He wrapped his sarong around his shoulders, but the little warmth it gave just made him yearn for his mattress and pillow all the more. On a house's front terrace, he saw a dog curled up on a heap of dirty rags, sleeping soundly, undisturbed. Deep in his heart, he wished he could curl up on that same pile of rags, just for a moment. Being a dog looked way better than being a child.

Tokkk-tokkk, dummm. Tokkk-tokkk, dummm. Some old man must've been weakly banging on the mosque's goatskin drum.

Then the call to prayer resounded from the Sowing the Seeds of Our Heavenly Land Mosque speaker and Father quickened his pace—he always tried to arrive at the mosque before the call was over. His sarong was tied at his waist, and one of his hands hiked the fabric up a bit, to keep it clean and to take wider steps.

As if there was a rope stretching from his father's body to his own, Sato Reang was always dragged along. If his father walked faster, he would walk faster. If his father turned right, soon enough so would he. If his father had decided to fly, Sato Reang believed he would find himself rising up into the sky.

He couldn't see his father quite clearly, the night turned him into a shadow which swayed to the rhythm of his footsteps in the pale streetlight. Sometimes the shadow disappeared, hiding in the shadows of houses and trees, but even so the rope that bound them together was always palpable. Ahead there were other shadows, also hurrying toward the mosque. Turning to look behind him, he could see two shadows more, side by side.

The father kept dragging Sato Reang, until he was standing in front of the mosque.

It's happening again, he thought suddenly, I'm a plastic ball. His body began to ache. He walked slowly toward the mosque terrace, following his father, and the pain intensified. The plastic ball was being sliced open, with that awful sound. *Nyit-nyit-nyit.* Sato Reang squeezed his eyes shut, but that didn't chase the pain away. Worse and worse, with every step he suffered. It's just a memory, he told himself. This is just a memory. My nauseating past.

Rotating with a few of the other mosque leaders, Father served as prayer imam. For pre-dawn prayers, their congregation was small. Only two lines of men and a line of women near the back. There were no children except for Sato Reang.

This time Sato Reang didn't know who would serve as the imam. He just let his feet keep walking, as he felt himself slowly being cut into two—hollowed, empty, gaping.

FIVE TIMES A DAY HE HEARD HIS FATHER'S VOICE REPEATING. FIVE times a day he was obliged to pray. It was God's orders. We're lucky that God didn't ask humankind to pray a thousand times a day, not even a hundred times, only five, and even then each time takes ten minutes at the most, usually less.

Even so, I always felt that five times a day was so many. This obligation was constantly stealing my time. Imagine, I've just fallen asleep and the banging on the door means I have to get up for pre-dawn prayers. After that, it's hard to fall asleep again, and sleep soundly, because I know that soon I have to get up again for school. And in school it's hard to muster up the energy to study in the morning, and once I've finally built up some enthusiasm near midday to learn something, here comes the call to prayer. After school, a hungry stomach pulls me to the kitchen, and I'm eating with gusto but just then, it's time for afternoon prayer. After that, going out to play with friends—riding bikes, swimming, or just walking around the market—suddenly the light is fading and the time to pray has come again. Then, not even two hours later, the fifth call to prayer resounds from the mosque.

I always felt that I hadn't yet had the chance to do anything. I could not do anything! Time never flowed freely—my time was torn to shreds, five times a day.

Occasionally I considered playing ball again, but to even think about it brought that sound to my ears, the machete hacking through plastic, and I'd lose the urge to go to the soccer field. One time, though now I was bigger, it crossed my mind to go to the rice fields. It was the dry season. I didn't need to buy crickets and fight them, I could just watch the little kids. But then I remembered Father looming over me.

'THIS SUNDAY, WE'RE GOING ON A PICNIC,' FATHER SAID ONE DAY. 'We'll all go,' he said. That meant Father, Mother, me, and my little sister, Kasih, who'd been born about two years after my foreskin was cut off.

A picnic! I never would have imagined that word coming out of Father's mouth. I'd heard about picnics from a few school friends, and one time the word appeared in a crossword puzzle. Finally! I thought. At long last, my life will be a little more colourful. I didn't ask any questions about where we were going—to climb a mountain, maybe visit an old temple, explore a city amusement park, I'd be satisfied with any of those, as long as I could experience another world, see how it felt to ride a tour bus. As long as there would be a memory for me to look back on.

We set out after pre-dawn prayers. Many folks from the Sowing the Seeds of Our Heavenly Land Mosque were going. Mother looked radiant. My little sister was hopping around in excitement. I didn't see anyone my age, but somehow that didn't clue me in.

Only about four hours later did I realize what this 'picnic' really was. We drove past the provincial limits and arrived at a city that was a little bigger than Stone Swamp. We pulled into a large parking lot in front of a huge, majestic mosque. There were other tour buses filled with groups from other towns, some all decked out in matching uniforms of brightly-patterned shirts, like pre-school kids. Confused, I looked around and caught sight of a large banner hung at the edge of the parking lot: 'Grand Prayer Recitation with Revered Elder Scholar Syekh Ruhayat Jamil.' It also had a picture of a wrinkly old man on it, looking like a guardian of the faith on the mosque calendars—the scholar himself.

Now I understood. After we'd spread out our bamboo mats on the empty land all around the mosque and gathered to eat our provisions, he'd lead us in prayer and then we'd listen to the guy talk. According to my Father, this was a picnic.

Afterwards I learned that, in addition to being a gigantic mosque, that was where Elder Ruhayat Jamil lived. There was also a madrasa for teenagers. I can't remember the name of the mosque, and I don't want to. I've also forgotten the name of our tour bus and what we brought to eat. If there's one thing I *do* remember from that picnic, which is why I remember the guy's name, it was my first meeting with a certain boy my age. Maybe a little older than me, about thirteen.

This is how it went: apparently, Father had joined the Revered Elder Scholar Ruhayat Jamil's prayer recitation a number of times before, both grand ones like this and smaller ones, and that's because Father knew his son, Kiai Maulana, who lived in Stone Swamp. Kiai Maulana didn't come with our group because he'd already been at his father's house for a few days, but at the picnic we were introduced to him and his family. The scholar took special pride in introducing his grandson.

A little awkwardly, I shook the boy's hand for the first time, as I heard his name.

'Jamal.'

And it turned out that we didn't just live in the same town—we went to the same school, even though we were in different classes. At first glance, I had him pegged: one day, when he was all grown up, people would call him Kiai Jamal. If fate was kind to me, and I made it to adulthood, someday I would see a big banner, hung on the fence of some big field, with 'Revered Elder Scholar Jamal's Grand Prayer Recitation' written on it.

I did not want to be his friend.

EARLY IN THE MORNING, AT SCHOOL, KIDS WERE CLUSTERED AROUND the table at the front of the classroom, waiting. This happened all the time—maybe the teacher was still doing something in the faculty room, or maybe he was still on his way to school. During harvest time, because so many of the teachers grew rice and other crops, they'd often come late, or sometimes not at all.

The group was talking about the soap opera that had aired the night before. Girls and boys alike were always getting swept up in the latest sad story, or its opposite, one so happy it had made them cry. A female friend was cursing a character for his infuriating behaviour—he hadn't done what he should have done, but, 'Well,' a male friend tried to explain, 'actually...'

I just listened, one bench behind them. I didn't really understand what they were talking about, didn't recognize any of the names they mentioned—that's right, because I hadn't watched the show! And not just the night before, I *never* watched it. A few others didn't watch either, but that was because they hadn't enjoyed it, and they still could happily chime in with taunts about what a garbage waste of time it was.

Not me. Because while everyone else was watching television (or doing something better with their time), I would be in the main room of my house, sitting at our large table, the Qur'an spread open before me. Father would be sitting on the sofa in the front room, smoking clove cigarettes, but he was listening closely. As I guided myself with a stick that I held like a pencil, I read the Arabic letters. Line by line. Verse by verse. Surat by surat. From the first page and onwards from there, every night—and if I decided to dedicate myself to true piety, I would read it over and over and over until the very end of my days.

I couldn't watch television anyway, because we didn't own a set.

That's why I never joined in my friend's conversation. I didn't know the shows, and I didn't know the actors.

Now school was almost over, and really we were just waiting for the bell to ring. A few kids had gone to the canteen, but I didn't have any money. Sitting at a slight distance on a chair in the corner, my body turned away toward the window, dying inside, I felt dumb for not having brought my crosswords. One of the teachers would inspect the children's backpacks, snatching out anything that wasn't a lesson book—magazines, novels, comics. But for some reason, crosswords were an exception. If he found the crossword booklet in my bag, he always just returned it to me.

Then someone knocked on the window next to my seat. I looked over and saw a face practically pressed up against the glass. Jamal.

His mouth was moving like a fish at the surface of the water, but I couldn't hear him or make out what he was saying.

Ah shit, I thought. I didn't want to be his friend and I resented his familiar air, just because we'd been introduced at his super famous grandfather's prayer event.

Jamal was strange. He didn't have any friends. Even though I rarely hung out with the other kids, I was still friendly with them. I would feel so weird if I associated with him. Plus, I'd noticed that he never raised his hand to salute the flag during our Monday ceremonies. He wouldn't recite Pancasila. One of our classmates said he never ate in roadside stalls because he couldn't be sure whether the food was truly halal. He wouldn't touch a female's hand in greeting.

Jamal knocked on the glass again and motioned for me to just come outside. So I went and could finally hear what he'd been saying: 'Let's go to the mosque. Let's pray.'

Damn.

Usually I said my midday prayers at home, after school, never at the school mosque.

I hesitated.

'You forgot, your father told me to make sure we said our midday prayers at school.'

That little monkey. He'd found my weak spot. I was worried he'd tell his father, and his father would tell my father. Powerless, I followed after him, knowing what people would think. Because it wouldn't just happen that day, but the day after that, and the next day, and the next, every day except school holidays.

I. Did. Not. Want. To. Be. His. Friend.

BUT DAMMIT ALL, AFTER I GRADUATED FROM MIDDLE SCHOOL, IT turned out Jamal had enrolled at the same high school—and, not just that, fate put us in the same class, and without checking with me first, he chose me for his seatmate!

Was this what they call the will of God?

In any case, now I was sixteen but not much had changed. I'd still never been to the movies, never had a girlfriend, though secretly I'd felt my heartbeat quicken as certain girls caught my attention. And the whole Jamal situation was worse. If I was there, he was too. If he wasn't there, then the likelihood was that I wouldn't be either. Because the school day now lasted through the afternoon, I *had* to pray at school—with Jamal, of course.

On Saturday nights, if anyone cared, I could be found riding on the back of Father's bicycle. My body was still so slight that Father had no trouble steering us around. The chain barely clicked because he greased it diligently, but you could hear the dynamo whirring. It connected to the lamp, which glowed yellow—sometimes bright, sometimes dim, according to how fast Father pedalled as we cut through the streets of Stone Swamp, which were never busy. My mother and my little sister would be up ahead, riding in a *becak* pedicab.

As we passed the market, which was always brightly lit out front, I would try to hide my face. I was worried I'd see my schoolmates—usually there were some girls gathered around the *bakso* meatball cart or in front of the arcade, with one or two of my old friends in the mix. I could imagine what they would say if they caught sight of me, 'Look at that! It's Sato Reang! He must be going to prayer recitation.' It would sting even worse if someone said, in earnest, 'It's good he and Jamal found each other. They make sense as friends.'

'The prayer house gang.'

'The pious kid syndicate.'

Even though the words came from inside my own head, I began to feel sorry for myself. You poor guy, I thought. I should get to try one of those games! I should get to wear my newest jeans, roll up my sleeves, and stand under the awning of a market stall, telling all kinds of jokes that make the girls burst out laughing.

The sad part was, I wasn't even sure I could tell jokes if I'd gotten the chance.

As we passed the town square, I hid my face more desperately. I'd caught a glimpse of two of my school friends walking together, exuding excitement and cheer. They were going to the movie theatre, no mistake. Mondays, they would talk in front of the school about the films they'd seen. I was nothing but a listener, the one who knew absolutely nothing, just as in my elementary school days I'd been the one who never watched television. I would never be anything but the strange kid who was awkwardly left out of most conversations until Jamal would come fetch me and take me to the school mosque to pray and read the Qur'an.

Don't let them see me. Don't let them talk about me. I was busting out of my skin, silently willing Father to pedal faster. I buried my head in his back, relieved once the bicycle arrived at the mosque yard.

For two hours, I was caged inside. There were only a few other kids, and they were much younger than me. If there was someone my age, you can guess who it was—Jamal. Always Jamal.

Sometimes I looked over at my mother, silently begging her, can't I just leave, can't I just go walk around with my friends, at the market or the town square? She would look back at me, but her expression gave no answer. Which meant: *You know that looks like that have to be addressed to your father.*

But I already knew what he would say.

I could keep feeling sorry for myself and I was sure I could still bear that for months to come. As long as no one else felt sorry for me.

WHAT WE CALLED THE MOVIE THEATRE AT THAT TIME WAS just a makeshift wooden structure, which in earlier days had been a stage for plays and *wayang orang* performances. But for years now, they'd been playing films there on Saturday night—maybe since before my foreskin was taken, or even before I was born.

I'd never been inside, let alone experienced the atmosphere when the lights went dark and a film started playing on the screen. Piecing together what my friends had said, I knew there were no chairs or seats, just rows of long wooden beams to sit on. During the film, snack and drink sellers would step among these rows, simply hopping over a beam to get to the next row. Smoke would billow throughout the space, mingling with the mentholated aroma of *minyak angin*, the cure-all massage oil.

Many times as a teenager I'd tried to find the opportunity to go there and watch a film, so I could talk about it with my friends Monday morning at school. I was always waiting on Saturday afternoons, just hoping Father would say, today we are not going to mosque for prayer recitation, because this or that Revered Elder Scholar who was supposed to come suddenly fell ill—I didn't care if some elder scholar had gotten sick or died, or a kyai had been hit by a car, or an ustaz had gotten invited to speak and recite prayers somewhere else for a larger fee, or if the mosque had been flattened in an earthquake, as long as Father told me that we weren't going to prayer recitation and I could slip out of the house and go to the movies.

But that had never happened. Somehow God always managed to guard the health and safety of all those scholars, kyais, and ustaz, so they never missed one single opportunity to share their wisdom and guidance.

At least I could sneak out to the night market, though I couldn't linger. After my routine of reading a few pages of the Qur'an and finishing my homework, I would head out, saying I was going to buy some snacks.

The night market was held on the military soccer field, and it was only open once a month on Friday, Saturday, and Sunday. I could go there on Friday or Sunday night. Of course there wasn't anything as exciting as a movie there, but at least I could watch someone do card tricks. Sometimes I'd run into friends and pretend I was also a normal kid, who went to the night market just like anyone else. They'd greet me with the slang of the time: 'All clear?' I'd reply 'All clear,' silently hoping that no one would then ask, 'You're not at prayer recitation?' A question like that, no matter what tone of voice it was asked in, always sounded like an insult. It would sting just as much if someone asked me, 'Where's Jamal?'

Those fools, did they think he was my identical twin? My life partner? My royal consort? I'd work myself into a state—evil thoughts would crowd into my head. I'd want to shove Jamal's face into the water trough in the school bathroom and send him to God's eternal dwelling place. But forget it, I would never actually do something like that.

On one of my visits to the night market, I saw a new ring toss game. You'd buy five rattan rings. On the table, a variety of prizes were laid out that you could aim for with the rings—a pack of cigarettes, a little doll, toy cars, a watch, even a box full of cash. I bought five rings hoping I would get a small teddy bear.

I didn't get the bear, but I did get a stuffed monkey. I was pretty proud of myself, because other folks had thrown ten, fifteen, or even twenty rings without winning anything. I went home happily and showed the monkey to my little sister Kasih. If there was one thing in this world that could be considered a consolation, it was her. She was such a cute kid, she was so sweet to me, and I utterly adored her. When I had extra money I happily indulged her in little snacks and treats. As I'd been tossing the rings, I'd been hoping to win something for her.

But when I held it out Father asked, 'Where'd you get that?'

I answered honestly. In my ignorance, I even went on about the sure-fire way to win a prize at the ring toss game, though my victory was likely beginner's luck. Father was not at all impressed. He snatched the little monkey away from my sister.

'That's gambling! A young kid like you, already wasting money on the devil's pastime!'

I gaped at him. My little sister gaped at him. I couldn't find my voice, couldn't say anything at all. Kasih also made no sound.

Father was playing with fire. He flicked his lighter and set the monkey ablaze. Right in front of Sato Reang and his little sister. The flames quivered and flared. Red. Yellow. Orange. A flicker of blue.

Now not only had I been severed in half along with a purple plastic ball, I also felt myself burning up with my little sister's stuffed monkey—and my soul began to thrash wildly in protest. And it kept on thrashing for a very long time.

RIDWAN HAD A GIRLFRIEND. AW HECK, I THOUGHT. THEN RANI had one. Damn. And in the following months a few more guys got girlfriends too. I thought, would it be so wrong if I did what they did? Sit close on a cafeteria bench, maybe sometimes holding hands? It seemed wonderful. As long as Father didn't find out. As long as Jamal didn't see, because everything he saw made its way back to Father.

A new kid moved to our town from the mountains. He quickly made friends and in a matter of days he had a girlfriend too. His name was Budiman. He sold magic charms that could make someone fall in love with you. Ridwan had bought one from him. So had Wijaya. So had Kusno. So finally I pulled out my money to buy one too.

It was just a small cloth sack with a bundle of roots inside, and I was supposed to put in some strands of hair from the girl I wanted. But I couldn't bring myself to say the name of the girl

I was secretly considering, I could only say she was my classmate.

One week, two weeks, three weeks. There was no sign at all that I was drawing her attention, or even if she'd noticed my existence or not. She acted just the same as always—in her eyes, I was just like anybody else. I complained to Budiman that his charm wasn't working. He told me to wait. Another week passed. Then two weeks, then three. I stopped complaining because I'd given up, but not totally—I stashed the charm in my closet, along with a little shred of hope, because who knows, maybe it would take effect when I least expected it.

But then another friend, Lukman, said to me, 'What would you even do if she did like you? How can you have a girlfriend if you can't go on dates? How are you supposed to invite her to walk around or go watch a movie if every Saturday night you're at prayer recitation?'

I felt like a bucket of shit had been thrown in my face. Shame, self-pity, and rage were all mixed up in my soul. I wanted to clench my hand into a fist and punch Lukman in the jaw, but I didn't have the strength to do it—plus, that shit that had come out of his mouth was the absolute truth, and I couldn't even tell whether he'd meant it as an insult, as an expression of sympathy, or maybe even as some kind of advice? I felt torn apart. I felt like I wasn't part of my gang of friends. I felt like I was nobody. But I wasn't riding on the back of Father's bicycle, so I had nowhere to hide.

They're infuriating, I thought. My friends are so infuriating.

Something was starting to burn inside my soul—though it was small, still just a spark. Had that spark come from my little sister's stuffed monkey getting set on fire?

SATO REANG KNEW HE'D NEVER BE ABLE TO GO TO THE MOVIE theatre on Saturday night. The universe was against him. But he could go there some other time, just like he'd gone to the night market. Just a moment there would be enough for him.

It finally happened, on the twelfth of October. Saying he wanted to go buy some chocolate cheese toast or a donut, he took his father's bicycle out of the shed and steered it toward the market but rode on past and turned to follow the dark road south.

The makeshift wooden structure that the kids called the movie theatre stood before him, deserted and shrouded in darkness, like a haunted house. Sato Reang stashed his bike under an almond tree by the side of the road, invisible even in the moonlight, and stealthily approached.

The door was unlocked. He went in freely and sat down on a bench, right in the center. So this is what it feels like to watch a film, he thought. The white screen seemed to emit its own pale glow. Everywhere else he looked it was murky and black. Darkness enveloped him.

For a moment, I was overcome with emotion—I was in the theatre! My eyes welled up. But I quickly returned to reality: no film was playing and I was alone. I wiped my eyes, vowing that one day I would be able to celebrate my freedom. One day, I'd be able to do whatever I wanted, and I could cry my heart out when that day came.

The darkness inside the movie theatre was total. No light came in. But then, suddenly, there was a spot of light in Sato Reang's hand. He slowly and carefully brought it to the front of the theatre. It flickered as he moved, and if it seemed it was about to go out, he'd stop until it was strong and steady again, and again he would advance.

At the front of the room, he held the light to the screen, which he realized was nothing but a large white sheet. The light began to grow, creeping across the cloth. He watched the light for a while before hurriedly backing up and slipping out, hopping on his bicycle, pedalling away. From a distance he could see the light growing, billowing out from the wood plank walls of the theatre. Then it shot out through the rooftop, illuminating a whole corner of the town. Sato Reang could hear people screaming, starting to run. Even years after, no one knew where the light—which had burned everything down to charcoal and ash—had come from, except Sato Reang.

And Sato Reang never again had to hear his friends gather around cheerfully discussing the films they'd seen. He'd learned from his father how fire obliterates.

NOW FATHER WAS LYING IN HIS GRAVE, NOT FAR FROM MY mother's mother, with worms and maggots keeping him company. Only a few steps from where my departed cousin had been laid to rest—he'd lived less than a year—and not far from the barber. He'd been our neighbour, and when he was alive he'd trimmed my hair whenever it started covering my ears and poking into my eyeballs.

'We all belong to God, and to God we shall return,' that's how it all started, with an incantation from the mosque loudspeaker. An announcement like that could only mean one thing: someone had just died. It would be followed with words like, 'Our relative has left this world…' Although the mosques didn't always have a tower, every mosque had a rooftop loudspeaker, to call people to prayer and to broadcast these announcements.

Then my uncle said, 'Now you're the only man in the house. You're taking your father's place.'

No, I muttered. No way. I would not take my father's place.

I would never hack up a purple plastic ball, I'd never split my own soul in two. Father was dead, and no one needed to replace him. But I didn't say this aloud, I just let these thoughts thunder around inside my head.

When they heard such announcements lilting from the mosque loudspeaker, people would fall silent for a moment. They would murmur a faint echo: 'We all belong to God and only to God we shall return.'

The women would start to move with a sense of urgency, gathering whatever they had in the kitchen cabinets—a few bundles of tea, a half pound of sugar, half a sleeve of cookies, a bag of coffee. They would wrap it up in a cloth, then they would step out of the house, their feet marking a determined path to the house of the bereaved.

The women always knew how to lighten each others' burdens. They would knock on the door, and without much conversation find a place to set down whatever they'd brought, then approach the wife who had been left behind, embrace her, pat her shoulder, and join in her wails and lamentations. They had the skill to bear some of her grief, but not just that. Without being told, their hands would begin to put the house back in order—straightening up the table and chairs, sweeping the floor, washing the dirty plates and glasses, boiling water for the tea or coffee for the people who would soon be coming to pay their respects.

Meanwhile a few men were gathering at the neighbourhood watch station. Two of them were wearing only shorts—no shirt, no shoes, the skinny one with dark skin, each holding a hoe. Others came with lengths of bamboo. An older man appeared with some packs of cigarettes, which quickly moved from one hand to another. The men would take one out of the pack and slip it between their lips before passing it on. Smoke billowed between them.

'Only yesterday he was out riding his bike. He stopped at my place to borrow a tire pump,' someone said.

'Pious people go easy. It happened after midday prayers, he was still in his sarong.'

They kept talking, only pausing to take deep drags on their cigarettes and exhale the smoke, and soon it became clear who would dig the grave, who would carve the grave marker, who would carry the casket, who would prepare the spot to bathe the corpse.

In every settlement there was a plot of land set aside for the dead. Everyone understood a day like this would come—no one knew who would be first and who next, but rest assured the empty land would end up filled, and once it was all full, they would dig it up again, turning over the earth where others had been laid to rest a long time ago.

A casket was also always waiting expectantly, on the terrace next to the mosque, knowing it would eventually be of use. Though no one knew just when, someone would surely lie down inside it, and four people with strong backs and thighs would surely carry it away.

The village leader would come to the family of the deceased, bringing a few yards of cloth for the burial shroud. He always offered it, knowing the dead villager would need it. Just as he himself would need it someday.

For a while, I still couldn't believe that Father was gone.

My whole life he'd always loomed larger than his physical body, which was short and slim—later, at his age, I'd be much taller. His forehead was a bit wide, and he'd cover some of it by growing out his hair in the front. I'd always thought he would live for a very long time. In fact, I hadn't been quite sure I'd ever have a life without him in it.

Even when they brought him to the mosque to pray over him for the last time, I still wasn't sure it was really him—his body looked tiny and frail, as if he'd already withered away.

It was only once I saw my mother and my little sister sobbing that I began to believe it.

My mother's brother took care of all the details of the funeral, working with the head of the neighbourhood and the mosque administrator, because they all thought of me as still too young; I was sixteen and apparently that meant I was useless.

At the top of the grave, Uncle placed a wooden grave marker with Father's name and family name written on it, and the dates of his birth and his death: Umar bin Abdul Malik, 1941-1991. Uncle also planted two frangipani saplings. They would grow tall and their crowns would grow lush, providing shade for Father's grave. Their dried-up leaves and flower petals would fall and adorn the mound of dirt, which still looked fresh and red.

'You must,' Mother urged me, 'replace that mound of dirt and wooden marker with proper stone and cement as soon as you can.'

I'd once heard someone say it's best to leave a grave simple, that a dead man didn't care whether his grave was grand and fortified with stone, because he was still dead.

But I didn't tell her so.

How old was he when he died? Forty-nine or fifty, it didn't

really matter, because it turned out that even my grandparents didn't know exactly when he was born. There were those who said he was too young to go. But people are born and they will most certainly die, and father was simply given one of the shorter turns on this Earth.

'Will mother remarry?' my little sister asked when the burial was done. We were both in the kitchen. There was no one there except us two. She was only seven. She looked exhausted from grief, from trying to hold back her tears. The poor thing, she was too little to lose her father. 'Will we have a stepfather?'

I wanted to say no, but then I hesitated. Mother was ten years younger than Father. She was too old to be a bride, but she also seemed too young to be alone, to have no more children. Who knows?

My sister's question had gotten me thinking. Would there be a new father? If so, would he hack apart a purple plastic ball? Would he burn a small stuffed monkey? What kind of man would approach Mother, what kind of man would Mother choose?

If Mother were to ask me whether she could remarry, I would definitely say no. But did a mother have to ask her children for permission to remarry?

'Brother?' My sister was waiting for my answer.

'I don't know.'

Mother was still greeting mourners. She wasn't crying anymore, or maybe she couldn't cry any more, but her eyes still looked red, puffy, and swollen. She'd used up a whole pack of tissues.

Not just our neighbours, but people from the market and outer settlements came. It seemed like Father had had many friends, and apparently some of them thought of themselves as more like family. And indeed, I'd heard Father say to people, 'We are family in faith, believe me.' I'd heard his friends greeting him, calling out, 'Ah, my brother!'

A few of them brought Mother white envelopes stuffed with cash, which she collected in a bag she held on her lap. This was the first I knew of people giving money to bereaved families, but after considering it, I thought, well maybe that's one way to comfort. To think of Mother experiencing a sudden windfall definitely made me feel better.

Still mulling over my sister's question, I took note of all the guests, especially the men—and although they were all there with their wives, I felt suspicious. I studied their faces, wondering whether they had a devious little plan to get a hold of my mother, though the dirt on my father's grave was still damp.

These thoughts kept spinning even as my classmates filed in. I had been in school when Father died and the class prefect had let me go home early. They must have collected money at school, and the prefect and the history teacher had brought the whole class to our house after the last lesson to offer Mother the money.

I felt a bit strange having my friends at my house.

They'd almost never come over before, except once or twice for something insignificant, like to borrow a book, or do homework together, and that had been only one or two kids. I didn't say anything to them, I didn't look any of them in the eye, although they greeted me, one by one, when they arrived.

Out of everyone who came, I just remember Ridwan, Agus, Salim, Jamal. And standing behind them I saw the girls, Ningsih, Rani, Bulan, Widyastuti. My childhood friend and neighbour,

Bunga, who'd always gone to the same school as me, also came. I stood there awkwardly as she hugged me. A few of them patted my shoulder. The class prefect also hugged me, but I could not shake my awkwardness.

The history teacher approached. He'd been a good friend of my father's. He said they'd gone to school together and had known each other since they were kids. He said to me, 'You're a pious child. Pray for your father. The prayers of a pious child open a pathway to heaven.'

Hearing him call me a pious child made me boil. That was when my thoughts returned of playing with fire. Maybe I would have to burn down the school, annihilate all my classmates, all my teachers.

AT A TIME BEFORE MY MEMORIES BEGIN, OF WHICH I COULD ONLY get a vague sense, based on what other people told me, Father had wanted to write silat stories. He'd amassed a collection of silat novels and comics—and tales of crime, romance, and horror—and even film adaptations. He turned the collection into a small lending library, and once he'd read the books himself he'd loan them out to school kids, the *becak* pedicab drivers, the truck and minibus drivers. He never lent out any book he hadn't read first, but only the silat stories assailed his brain. He told everyone he knew that he was going to write his own.

He bought a typewriter from a thrift shop at the market—a big machine with tiny letters, only about 10 picas, still plastered with a label proclaiming it the property of the sub-district office. They must have replaced all their equipment with newer, lighter, more compact models that were becoming popular at the time. On that typewriter, every night, he tried to bring forth the masterpiece he imagined.

'No,' my mother would say whenever I asked her, 'I don't remember him writing stories like that.'

I often tried to picture my father as a silat writer, but every time I failed. Whenever I tidied up the house, I would search for proof that he'd been one, but I never found any.

Maybe Mother's right, I thought. After all, a real silat writer would be nothing like Father. I'd always only ever known him as the kind of man who went to mosque and became prayer leader and gave sermons from the pulpit during Friday prayers. There's no way he was a silat writer, not even a talentless one.

But Aunt and Uncle said the typewriter would be click-clacking away in the little library every night back when my parents were newlyweds—which was kind of long ago, yet they spoke about it as if it were still fresh in their minds. I began to wonder whether Mother had truly forgotten, or whether she just didn't want to remember, and didn't want to talk to me about it.

Uncle said Father's first efforts produced two hundred pages, but these only disappointed him. The main character was a drunken warrior who was followed around everywhere by a faithful monkey; when Father realized this was too much like other silat stories he'd read he worried people would think it was at best derivative and at worst plagiarism and he burned the manuscript. Plus, he'd told my aunt, the story was boring. I could certainly imagine that! A story as boring as its author.

I only began to believe the truth of my aunt and uncle's stories when one day, Father brought me to our neighbour the barber. A new market had been built, on empty land studded with a few almond trees. They'd also opened a food stall, a cockfighting arena, and a guard post, and he'd found a spot for a barber shop.

Father left me with the barber, going to the market to buy something.

My style never changed much—short with a small quiff in the front—so the barber got started and as he worked with his comb and scissors, occasionally spraying my hair with water, he reminisced, 'I used to read your father's silat stories.'

It took a moment for that to sink in.

After his first failed attempt, Father stayed away from the typewriter for a few weeks, before going to the stationary shop and coming home with two reams of paper. At that time, Mother was pregnant with their first child, and the typewriter clattered away almost every night. Click-clack. Click-clack. Click-clack-click-clack. Sometimes he wrote almost until dawn, only stopping when he heard the call to prayer. Uncle said even back then he never skipped his prayers, but he hadn't yet become a mosque administrator.

I told Uncle that the barber had read Father's silat stories, and he chuckled.

'Yeah, yeah,' he said. 'Yeah, he must've. Your dad was a regular customer, he probably brought a story or two with him whenever he went for a trim.'

'Were Father's stories ever made into a book, ever published?'

Uncle shook his head.

He said that after his fourth or fifth attempt Father didn't set his writing on fire, and in fact he felt confident enough to have it bound. And then he slipped it in with the other books he loaned out. Father figured if it turned out lots of folks liked it, he would send it to a publisher—he'd already made note of some addresses printed on the backs of his silat books. But sadly, while some borrowed it, only a handful read the whole thing, and none of them came to him with eyes wide and shining, having just read a tale that had blown their minds.

Father was devastated. He stopped talking about silat stories so much. The typewriter fell silent—if it did start clacking, he was likely writing something else.

His declining interest extended to the lending library. If someone had borrowed a book and didn't return it for days and days, Father no longer went to the borrower's house to track it down. One by one, his books disappeared, and now all the multi-volume silat series were incomplete, missing titles.

Father didn't try to replace them, nor did he buy any more books, though people would ask about new releases. He never went into the library anymore, though it was set up on the front terrace of his very own house.

There was a new library in a corner of a nearby city and the regulars slowly trickled away and started going there. Finally, people stopped coming altogether.

For years after I heard that, I thought maybe there were still some books leftover. I'd look for them but I never found any. I became convinced that after Father had decided to close his lending library once and for all, the books disappeared—maybe he'd sold or donated them. By the time he'd closed the library, his ambition of being a silat story writer was gone.

And that was around the time when Mother gave birth to their first child. The only thing that was left in Father's dreams of writing silat stories was the name of the warrior, which he'd used in every one of his manuscript drafts.

A week after the baby was born, someone asked Father, 'And what will you name him?'

Yes, Father had gotten a boy: me. And he decided to bestow the warrior's name upon his offspring.

'Sato Reang,' Father said.

After Father's death, I didn't go back to school, because I was still fantasizing about burning it down—I obsessed and ruminated over how I would do it, what day of the week would be best, and how to make sure that no one would find out that I was the one who'd done it. It hounded me, the urge was too powerful, I couldn't even get near the building.

One morning, I was sitting on the back terrace, watching Father's chickens make a fuss in the yard. They were starving, because Father was the one who'd fed them. Maybe they were wondering where he was.

They wandered all over the place, clucking and squawking, running along the bamboo fence to the kitchen door—waiting for Father to come out.

He'd prepare a sack of feed, which he'd bought from the rice mill. Every morning, for years, he would pour some feed into a small bucket, then add some hot water and stir it up. The steam would waft up, fragrant with the aroma of rice. That was the chickens' breakfast.

Without thinking too much about it I prepared their food as I'd seen Father do it so many times. I looked out at the chickens, then called them. But at that instant, I felt Father enter my body, possess me against my will. I shouldn't have fed them, I should have let them find their own food or starve to death.

Go Father, I said. Go. Go. Go!

I kicked over the small bucket of chicken feed, screaming 'Go! Go! Go!'

'There are lots of mice on the trellis,' my little sister said. She'd heard them running across, making a ruckus when the neighbour's cat jumped onto the roof.

'Let's see,' I said, 'whether any got caught.'

If anyone didn't miss Father, it was these mice. Every night, Father would set traps on the roof and in the storehouse, the kind that snaps its serrated teeth into the trapped rat like a shark, breaking its back.

Before bed, I had set some, using peanut butter as bait, just as Father used to do.

I looked up at the trellis. A rat was in its death throes. I brought it down and my little sister said, 'You're just like Father.'

No. No I am not.

I wanted to shove that rat corpse right down her throat.

DEAD OR STILL DYING, FATHER WOULD PUT THE TRAPPED RATS in a bucket and bring them to the yard behind the house, where there was a trash heap, in a big dug-out pit, hidden from view by some clusters of banana trees. He'd throw household trash there, and the dry leaves he'd gathered off the ground, and the dead, hanging banana stalks he'd chopped off at the stem.

There, he lit a fire, letting it consume everything dry, heat up everything wet. At times like that, our neighbour on the right would open the door to the bamboo gate, bringing trash from his own house, and then stand there chatting with Father. They looked like boy scouts at a bonfire. Soon their nostrils would start flaring, then they'd start chuckling.

'It always smells so good.'

'Burned rat flesh smells just like grilled goat.'

'But we don't know what it tastes like.'

'We don't know,' Father said, 'And we don't ever need to know.'

HE ONCE WAS A FISHERMAN, THIS NEIGHBOUR OF OURS. BUT AS HE got older, his hands and feet suffered from rheumatism. He could no longer go to sea and endure the damp night air. Now he lived alone in a small house just across the alley, working to repair other fishermen's nets. He also made and sold fish bait. As long as he didn't have to come in contact with the ocean air, he was happy.

Every morning at the trash heap he'd chat with Father. On Wednesday nights, they also had the same shift on neighbourhood watch, with four other men. When it was his shift, the fisherman would usually bring his carrom board table, and Father would help him carry it down the alley toward the security post. The carrom seeds were in a cloth pouch hanging from his waist. Father would provide baby powder to lubricate the surface of the table.

They would play until just before dawn, when Father would

go say his prayers. They'd chase away the boredom as they waited their turn to patrol the neighbourhood, so everyone could sleep soundly without being bothered by thieves, free from worries of wayward sparks. They'd play carrom without betting on the game.

I knew this old fisherman pretty well myself. In the afternoons on the way home from school sometimes I'd flop down on the shabby old chair out on his front terrace. It was the most comfortable place to lie for a bit, shaded from the sun by the lush canopy of mango trees that grew beside his house.

Once he realized I was on his terrace, the old fisherman would usually appear with a small glass jar filled with peanuts and sit beside me. His head was full of stories; occasionally one would come out, and I was always ready to listen.

It's possible that my dream of paddling a skiff in the middle of the wide ocean came from him, because never once in my life had I gone far from shore. I only knew the edge of the sea, I'd never swam past the breaking waves nor had I ever ridden in a skiff, let alone steered one myself—I don't know how I had such skill in my dreams.

When he was a very young man, he'd been pierced by a stingray's tail and haemorrhaged. The hull was red with his blood. He thought his time was drawing near. He begged a friend to throw his corpse overboard, saying it would be an honour for a fisherman to be eaten by the fish.

But somehow he survived. Their boat had an engine, and his friends raced as fast as they could for shore. They carried him to the health center, unconscious. There was no doctor, but a nurse was able to save his life.

Without the hope of such stories, I never would have sat on

the terrace of his house, though I must admit he didn't speak to me much. He more often spoke to Father, and now he had lost his trash heap campfire companion.

I HAD ALSO EAVESDROPPED ON HIS LOVE STORY.

Long ago, when he was a very young man, he'd occasionally gone to sea alone—if his friend was sick, say, and he couldn't find a replacement. That was fine. The ocean is the only friend a fisherman needs. He loved the sea and he always aimed to catch more fish than the others, even when he had on deck only his own two hands.

'You don't need to be so greedy,' advised the older fishermen. 'Be happy with a small catch, Barkah. Spend your time and energy looking for a girl, go fall in love.'

He just laughed. He didn't need a sweetheart. He'd watched as a few of his friends had found women—they'd grown whiny and soft. Out on the water all they talked about was these women of theirs, about how they longed to return to port as quickly as possible, how their yearning and desire was pulling them back. It was boring talk, they caught less fish, and they wasted the small amounts of money they got from the smaller catch buying little presents at the night market. Love turned men into fools, and he didn't want to fall into the pit they had dug. With his persistence, despite his simple way of life, he was able to buy a plot of land and build a small house a little ways from the beach, where he'd move once he got older and needed some distance from the ocean's shivering winds. He spent some of his other profits on a new engine and a reinforced hull. He planned to keep saving up for a new boat with an outboard motor. He'd find someone to drive it, and they'd split the proceeds from the catch. In ten or fifteen years, he'd be a boss.

'Look, Barkah,' the older fishermen said. 'Your friends have all married, one by one.' But just as before, he only chuckled. He'd seen those friends alright. By their wedding days the romance had already faded, and things got worse from there. There were always mouths to feed back at the house, whether or not they caught as much as they'd hoped for. At first it was just one mouth, then two, then soon enough three, and the number would keep growing if they didn't do something to put a stop to it. Their wife and children became a source of resentment. These friends would go down to the beach not to work, but to escape, yet the mouths at home still clamoured for food. His friends were forced to go to a middleman, asking for money up front. Once the catch came in, they'd have to give the middleman the fish, and so no longer had money in hand. It was even more complicated when the money lender came into the picture. They paid off their debt by selling fish, but they could never truly break even. Their faces wrinkled up. Grey hairs poked out. The fire in their eyes had begun to flicker and die.

Was that the kind of life he wanted, the life his friends had? No. A woman, a marriage, could wait.

'You need someone to massage your tired muscles,' the old fishermen kept cajoling. Some of them even offered a few young women they knew. He shook his head no, not interested. Besides, he thought, surely women didn't get married just to become some man's masseuse and keep his body warm at night.

BARKAH THE FISHERMAN CONTINUED HIS SOLITUDE. HIS ONLY companion was his boat. There were boys who would apprentice themselves to him, but they'd get sick, or they'd have too much homework, and so he'd return to the sea alone.

Until one night full of blessings.

That night, he saw only one other boat. This struck him as strange. Usually there were many—even in the fog he could make out their lights, glowing in the distance. But that night he only saw one light, not too far away. He didn't recognize the vessel. The sea was calm, there was no sign of rain or a storm. He decided to approach.

It turned out the boat had just one young woman sitting in it. He thought maybe it was a sea devil, and prepared to flee. But, when in a momentary flash of lantern light they locked eyes, the fisherman was ensnared. He'd fallen in love.

The woman caught very few fish. It was clear she'd been to

sea—maybe a fisherman's daughter—but she wasn't very skilled. Barkah stayed with her the whole night, worried some disaster would befall her, showing her what she needed to do. In the faint pre-dawn light, Barkah offered her half his catch.

At first she refused.

'You need those fish more than I do,' Barkah said. 'You wouldn't be out here on the ocean all alone if you didn't.'

The woman softened at his words and headed back to shore.

They met again a few times after that, always at sea. They'd return to the same spot, each in their own boat, finding a way to distance themselves from the other fishermen. Barkah would keep her company, chatting, coaching her, and sharing his catch. As the days passed, they began to tie their boats together with a rope. One day, the fisherman leapt into the woman's boat. Their hearts raced, they trembled, but not from the chill sea air.

The seeds of love that had been planted with their first glance took root, then spread like a vine, blossomed with abandon.

But unfortunately for them, the woman already had a husband back on shore. He'd been gravely injured in an accident. The woman, who had inherited fisherman's blood from her father and her grandfather, decided to push her boat into the water. She would have to feed herself, and the man who could no longer do anything except open his mouth.

Their relationship continued for weeks—far from shore, far from other people. They would sit in the boat, in each other's mournful embrace.

'What can I do? I would never leave him,' the woman said.

The fisherman could only hold her close.

Then one night a storm raged. 'Maybe this was my punishment, or hers,' the fisherman would say to whoever would listen, as if confessing his sins. His baby was growing in her womb, she was four months along. They were weeping, trying to devise a plan for the future, when a huge wave crashed into them, splitting the hull and capsizing their skiff.

Amidst the pouring rain, the rioting waves, the dark sky, he couldn't see her. He screamed and yelled, caught a glimpse of her hand and tried to reach for it, but another wave drove them apart. He was able to grab onto an empty jerrycan that had been thrown from her boat as it floated past him, but he never saw his beloved again.

She'd been swallowed by the ocean.

After that, he lost all his ambition. He didn't want to buy another boat. He didn't care about trying to catch more fish than the other fishermen. He ended up becoming the opposite of his friends—he'd lost his lust for the sea not because he was drained by the gaping mouths at home, but because he knew there would be no one waiting for him back on shore. Now he sailed just to remember their time together, nothing more.

He never married. He lived alone until his old age. Shipwrecked by a tsunami of love.

'YOU WEREN'T SAD, WHEN YOU DECIDED THAT YOU'D GONE TO sea for the last time?'

Sato Reang forgets who asked Barkah that. As a kid, Sato Reang could only listen.

'I was sad, but I had to stop.'

'But how could you bear to keep yourself away?'

Turns out that was another story. After years of going out to sea, always longing for the open ocean but also his beloved, he felt the time had come. His body was giving out, his vision was starting to blur, his bones were starting to creak and groan.

That night at sea, at the exact spot where he was sure that they used to meet and make love, he sat there lost in thought the whole night long. He would never come here again. His time was up. And to make sure of it, he started to strip off his clothes. Like most fishermen, he wore many layers to keep warm but now he stripped them all off. He dropped the clothes in a heap at the bottom of the boat. Barkah took a jerry can filled with benzine, then poured it out onto the pile. He removed the engine and placed it in the middle of the boat.

He threw himself into the water. Still holding onto the side of the boat with one hand, he used his other to reach for the lighter he had ready, and he set the clothes on fire. Flames ignited, slowly growing.

He swam for shore, offering himself to fate. If he was to tire and drown, he would be together with his beloved once more. If he survived, the universe had given him just a little more time to tell their love story.

Hypothermia was setting in and Barkah was starting to sink when a fisherman saw his burning boat and saved him.

I think old Barkah's tale of burning his boat embedded itself in my soul. And then too, I'd seen for myself how the flames consumed my little sister's stuffed monkey. I loved fire. I'd heard too that in hell God had entrusted fire with the task of burning off sins.

IN THE MORNING, AS I WAS BURNING TRASH (INCLUDING THE RATS THAT I had pulled from the traps), I saw him emerge from his house. He opened the bamboo gate, carrying a basket half full with garbage, then approached me. Without saying much—as if we had done this often, he and I—he squatted beside me and tossed the garbage from his basket into the lick of flame.

'People come and go,' he said. I didn't know who he was talking about. Father, or his beloved who had died at sea? 'At first it will be quite difficult but as time passes, you'll find your body and soul can bear the loss.'

I didn't reply.

'When I looked out, I thought I saw your father burning trash. Turns out it was you.' So it was true. Father's soul was still wandering and now it had possessed me. Against my will, he'd made me do everything that he used to do.

Barkah had burned his boat. What would I have to burn to distance myself from Father, who was still with me all the time, even after his death?

THERE WAS A SMALL POND, JUST SEVEN FEET BY TEN, NOT FAR from the trash heap. It was filled with wastewater from the kitchen and the toilet—water that had been used to wash the glasses and plates and was carrying left-over sauce and soup, used cooking oil, old tea, mixed with soap and detergent and urine.

Father had thrown catfish eggs in there. Once hatched, they were tough, real fighters, surviving in that water. It was beyond murky; it was a rank, filthy black. The thick layer of sludge at the bottom seemed to replenish itself even though the pond was dredged twice a month.

I was not Father.

I didn't need to trap rats. I didn't need to bring those rats to the trash heap and burn them while chatting with the old fisherman. And I didn't need to throw the burned rats—whose flesh maybe tasted as savoury and delicious as roasted goat—into the pond. So I left those rats in the trash heap—and their rotting stink filled the air.

The catfish in the wastewater pond had grown very large. They were ferocious, they would eat anything. Burned rats were their favourite. The instant Father would come stand at the edge of the pond, they were already jostling each other, headbutting, trying to jump highest out of the water.

But no, I would not give them that happiness. I would let them starve, become cannibals. The strong would eat the small, until there was only one left and he would eat himself. His mouth would open to swallow his tail, slowly, and then his body, and then he would eat his own head—his mouth chewing up his own mouth.

Go, Father. Be gone. Be gone from my body and be gone from my soul.

When Mother asked me to get rid of Father's things, I did it happily. I'll burn them, I thought. Fire would scorch all that remained.

Mostly, it was clothes. Mother had already sorted through them. Those still in good condition would be given to the less fortunate—*becak* pedicab drivers, market coolies, and grasscutters would all happily accept them. The rest, which Father had worn to chop down banana trees and were ripped and covered with sap stains, I threw in the trash pit.

I lit the fire and instantly the flames were dancing, leaping up out of the pile of clothes. There were a few small explosions, and a piece of scorched fabric was blown up into the air.

Back in the storage shed, I found two cardboard boxes filled with old magazines. I immediately recognized them as da'wah magazines for the proselytizing of the faith. If I'm not misremembering, they came once a month, and whenever the postman brought one, Father would take it and sit right down on the front room chair, read it very slowly and then leave it on the side table to re-read the next day.

I'd peeked inside them once or twice. There was not one single interesting thing to be found. There were almost no pictures, except for a few boring black and white photographs and a few cartoons that, to me, looked like they'd been made by people who didn't know how to draw. The cartoons in my crossword magazines were way better drawn and of course, way funnier.

Mother had told me that there was a trash picker who would take them—in fact, he was willing to buy them, paying by the kilo, but Mother had decided to give them to him for free. It was really a shame. I wanted them to burn, I wanted to watch the flames flicker and flutter. But I wasn't totally out of luck. Underneath the magazines I found other documents—sheets and sheets of paper with typewriting on it. Were these the silat stories I'd been looking for all these years? Had I finally found the adventures of the roving warrior named Sato Reang, the Sato Reang who was me? But even in this simple matter, Father let me down.

I slowly read the sheet of paper in my hand. It was entitled, 'Ten Material Temptations of The Faithful.' Ah, I remembered Father also often wrote out his Friday sermons. On Thursday nights, I would hear him typing, the sound echoing through the night click-clack, click-click-clack, click-clack-clack-clack. Yes, he'd kept the typewriter even though now he used it for other things. After just a few lines, I realized this wasn't a sermon. It was more like an article in a da'wah magazine. Maybe he'd submitted it to one of them, though I'd never seen or heard of any of them getting published.

Underneath it I found some more writing. 'The Prayer House and the Education of Muslim Children.'

Suddenly I pitied him. After failing to become a silat writer, he had also failed to become the writer of da'wah magazine articles. After rummaging around a bit, I found the return envelopes. The highlight of his career had been to give Friday sermons in a small mosque in a far corner of some small city.

Ignoring my mother's request, I burned those articles. If the magazines hadn't wanted them, let the fire prey upon them, take them out of existence. Everything he thought could disappear without a trace. The words he had put down to paper, the fruit of his fingers' hard work, would also become dust that returned to dust.

But still Father didn't disappear so easily.

One morning, because I didn't know what else to do, I rode my father's bicycle to the market. I went to park it in a bicycle lot. The place was still empty, only about five bicycles were leaning against the row of wooden stakes. I pushed the front wheel in between the stakes, then locked it with a chain. When I looked over, the old man guarding the lot was staring at me, pale, and starting to back away. I was about to ask him what was wrong when he said, 'Oh! I thought you were your father. I know that bicycle very well.'

Dammit, I thought. I should have walked.

But it didn't end there. Because I still didn't know what to do in the market that early in the morning, I went to the stall that sold pancakes and fried snacks. I sat on the bench and ordered a glass of *bajigur*. The old lady smiled at me as she poured my hot, creamy drink.

'That's just where your father used to sit.'

I could not get around the fact that many people in this small city had known my father. And this meant his spirit—which to me had been like a black shadow that was everywhere, spying on me, telling me what I had to do and what I was not allowed to do—hadn't been laid to rest along with his corpse. Though his body was buried and already slowly decomposing, people seemed to mention him all the more often—and not just that, they started talking to me as if Father had borrowed their mouths to speak through. They began looking at me as if Father had borrowed their eyeballs.

The pancake seller had gone on about what Father used to say until it made my ears ring. As she was stirring the pancake batter in the bowl on her small table, she looked as if she were hacking open a purple plastic ball. As she was adding fuel to the fire in her little oven, I was watching her burn a stuffed monkey. I felt a scream building up inside me, and so before I let it out I paid for my food and drink and hurried away without another word, leaving the pancake half eaten and the *bajigur* cooling in its glass.

FOR A WHILE I JUST WALKED AROUND THE MARKET, WITH NO particular destination in mind. It wasn't so early anymore, so I didn't come across any school kids getting on the bus out in front of the market, though I did see a few people I recognized, who asked me why I wasn't going to school. I gave a little smile but didn't answer. On my way back to the bike parking lot, I ran into a middle-aged man whose name I couldn't remember. He was friends with Father and I'd often seen him at Saturday night prayer recitation.

I wanted to turn around, but it was too late. So now the man before me would transform into Father, risen from the grave. I felt sick.

'Ah, how are your mother and little sister?' he asked, then mumbled apologetically that he had just gotten back from travel outside the city and hadn't yet had the chance to visit and extend his condolences.

'Fine.'

My reticence turned to suspicion. Why was he asking about my mother? Was he really going to come to the house? I was reminded of my little sister's question. Had this Uncle here thought of Mother the second he learned of Father's death? Was he hoping to marry her? Had he been interested in Mother this whole time? My mind was in chaos.

'You know, I'd never be where I am today without your Father.'

I half-listened as he told his story. A few years ago, when he was still a low-ranking employee at an ice factory, he'd received an inheritance from his parents. He asked Father what he should do with it; in fact, he wanted to sell at the market, but he didn't know what to sell. He wanted to be his own boss, and he was worried that once he quit his job, if he didn't use the inheritance as capital, it would quickly evaporate. Father advised him to sell cheap plastic home goods. Plastic plates, plastic cups, plastic chairs. Cheap ones, Father emphasized. At first, he wasn't sure, because at that time people didn't really eat or drink with plastic plates or cups, but he took Father's advice, and that day when I came across him in the parking lot, I could tell that he was one of the richest merchants in our market.

'If you need anything at all, please come see me at my house. Think of me as your own father.'

My own father! I wanted to burn down every kiosk in the market. I was nauseated, sick. I felt so sick.

NOW SATO REANG ISN'T SURE WHETHER HE SHOULD BURN DOWN the market or the school. The market would definitely be more complicated, because there were always people there, no matter the time of day or night, it would be almost impossible to avoid them—and if he succeeded, some might die. He didn't want to kill anyone, he just wanted to burn the market down, to see the giant flames. He just wanted to see all of that man's efforts, the plastic cups and plates he was so proud of, all the praise for his father's good advice, scorched and melted.

It seemed easier to burn down the school, because, like the theatre, the school was only guarded by one night watchman. But he worried that burning down the school wouldn't eradicate his father from his life.

He wasn't sure of any of it, really. Fire could easily turn the market, the school, anything, into charred debris. But his

Father would simply rise from the ashes, like a phoenix reborn. Whispering to him.

'You are a pious child. It's time to pray.'

Dokk-dokk! Dokk-dokk! Just like all the other long nights that had come before, Sato Reang heard the banging on the door. He'd learned to give a quick, 'Yes!' and so that stuttered call came of its own accord, even as he was still trying to regain consciousness. His eyes were open, but all he saw was fog as his body picked itself up and his two feet swung over the side of the bed. He yawned, gradually becoming aware of his surroundings—his room, what time it was. He shifted his weight to make his bed creak as if he'd gotten up.

Slowly he came out of his room, prepared to see his father there. Father always waited for him to emerge, waited for him to wash his face, waited for him to pull on his sarong, then together they would leave. And that's what he was doing, as he'd done for years. Every movement was inscribed into every muscle of his body, he did all of it without thinking. Sato Reang opened the door soundlessly, walked through the small alley that separated his house from the old fisherman's house, past the neighbourhood watchpost out front. From there he walked, under the shadow of night and through the cold morning air, toward Sowing the Seeds of Our Heavenly Land Mosque. With every step there was that familiar sound. *Nyit-nyit-nyit.* The blade of a machete severing a plastic ball.

He was already standing there in the mosque yard when he realized he hadn't been following his father. He'd thought he'd heard his father banging on the door, he'd thought his father had been waiting, he'd thought he'd been following his father to the mosque.

But Father wasn't there anymore. Father was dead. Then it hit him: he didn't need to burn down the market or the school to exorcize his father's ghost. All he had to do was stop going into the mosque. Stop praying. Stop trying to please, and start distancing himself from whatever his father had taught him. He would refuse to be a pious child.

I decided to keep walking toward the city, past the pale yellow streetlights. I'd left my house for the mosque but for the first time, I didn't go inside. 'What for,' I thought, 'if I'm not going to pray?'

For the first time in a long, long time, my spirit felt weightless—as light as a kapok blossom floating on the wind, a sure sign of the coming rain.

I SWEAR, ON THE STINK OF SEWAGE, THIS IS WHAT I DID NEXT TO celebrate my freedom. I pissed into the back of a pickup truck. My piss rained down upon its haul, wooden crates filled with apples and pears.

It was getting near dawn. I knew the pickup would be there, in front of the still-shuttered fruit store. Who knows where the driver or young navigator had gone, maybe they were sleeping somewhere more comfortable, or chatting in a coffee stall. As usual, they'd gotten here too early—the fruit couldn't be unloaded and brought into the shop before daylight, so they would just leave their full truck there, trusting in their fellow man. But I'd stolen an apple one morning when I was wandering toward the market after pretending to go to Subuh prayers at the mosque, and two pears another night.

At first I had just intended to steal one more apple. It was so easy to pull back the tarpaulin, and I was sure no one would notice. The streetlights were dim, the driver must have been at least a couple blocks away. I was trying to break off one of the crate's wooden slats when I got a better idea. An astonishing, confounding idea. An idea that champed at the bit, begging to be brought to life, begging to bring me even farther astray from Father's demand for piety. So instead of stealing an apple or pear, I ended up pissing on cartons of them, spewing out as much as I had in me.

Someone would buy one of those apples or pears at a fruit stall. I hoped the stall owners would be too lazy to wash the fruit or even wipe it down before setting it out for display—which seemed pretty likely, their lives were exhausting with never-ending work and responsibilities. Then someone would bring it home, stash it in their refrigerator or fruit basket. Then, one afternoon, someone in the household would pick it up. Bite it. Lick it. Chew it. Swallow it. They would be grateful to me for its unique aroma, which would have mellowed over time. For its certain taste when they chewed the peel. For its extra nutrition. To your good health, my friend. Above all, they had already given me a little joy. Just a little. They didn't know me, a random sixteen year old, and I didn't know them, but at least I had given them just a bit of me.

I must admit, Sato Reang had often thought that he was of little use to the world—despite all the pretence to make Father and Mother happy, they somehow knew he could never make them proud. In truth, Sato Reang felt like paint on a wall. It was there, but nobody cared at all.

For months after that, though, I still couldn't sleep much at night. In the early hours, I'd hear that '*Dokk-Dokk-Dokk!*' though

I knew there was no one at my door. Maybe I would always hear it. One night, for the first time in my life, I tried sleeping at the neighbourhood watchpost. But even there I heard it and startled awake with a gasp—even after death, Father was trying to get me up for pre-dawn prayer. No, Father, I won't do it!

Wearing a ratty old sweater for warmth, I'd leave the house and walk along the city alleyways, hoping the night wind would soothe me, distract me from my insomnia until my eyelids started to droop and my feet began to drag. These walks took me past the parts of the city that were dead, dark and silent, the inhabitants enjoying a well-deserved sleep before having to get up the next morning and hurry to the factory, to school, to the shops, to dull government offices. But in other neighbourhoods, the city still had a pulse. In front of the market, guys were breaking down the boxes they'd used to haul their vegetables. Some security guards were playing cards in the parking hut. A few customers were gathered in the coffee stall. A vagrant was pawing at a garbage pile.

I never approached anyone. I didn't feel the need, and it was clear they didn't need me—they didn't even notice me as I passed by. I just needed to walk, to tire myself out. By morning's light, I would be so exhausted that I could finally go home and sleep, just as my old friends were starting to jostle each other on their school bench. Ha ha ha. Suck it up.

I meandered along the deserted roadsides. Walking past a bus stop shelter, the colourful cluster of advertisements and announcements plastered one atop the other on its wall caught my eye. I stopped to read a few. 'House demolition services available,' that's what one of them said. Imagine how useful people like that are—without them, how could anyone get rid of a dilapidated house full of memories they were hoping to quickly forget? How else, on that patch of earth, could someone hope to build a new house and the new life to go with it? 'Need your septic tank pumped out? Contact us.' Extraordinary. There were those who wanted to deal with other people's shit. Without them, there would be plenty of washrooms splattered with sewage that had been building up for years until it burped up out the squatty toilet hole and went splodging across the washroom floor. And imagine, without people willing to suck up the sewage from its tank, the people in this city would have to go back to shitting into the river, or squatting on a board set jutting out above an irrigation ditch. No river or ditch? They would learn from the feral cats, digging a hole in the yard somewhere—and don't forget where you'd buried the last pile, because if you went digging into the same hole your little trowel might stir up the old pungent stuff.

Suddenly I remembered when Kurnia had thrown that plastic bag full of shit into the city minibus. I missed my childhood, and I missed my school friends.

Aw hell!

I'm not sure when I first saw the pickup. The driver and navigator were gone and I casually lifted the tarp to see what was inside. I'd already started walking away when I felt the urge to steal—just one apple, I thought. As far as I remembered, I'd probably stolen a few things before but it wasn't some grand theft that anyone knew or talked about, and it had been a very long time ago. Other people had stolen everything from me, so why not try taking something back? One apple wasn't anywhere near what I'd lost. They wouldn't miss it.

Eating the stolen apple as I walked back to my house, I felt so happy—a feeling which had become alien to me, after days spent choking with anger. For some reason I felt righteous. If the store owner suffered the loss of one apple, I would simply say: see how it feels? You should thank me for giving you that feeling. I've been overwhelmed by an abundance of it, now we can share.

After some time passed I did it again, two more times, and the same feeling permeated my entire body each time. It occurred to me that I could spend the rest of my life, which maybe wouldn't even last that much longer, as a petty thief. Darn, I should have started a long time ago, when I was a kid, like Tongos, the little market stealer. Where was he now? I had wanted to be like him, but as with many things in my life, I had failed to manifest even such a simple desire. But it's alright, I told myself. As the wise men say, better late than never.

It was a dog that changed my plans to steal another apple—I mean, maybe I would have still stolen a few more, just for my own sense of justice, but this dog gave me a better idea. And I guess, if you really thought about it, that's just how I was. At my age—when most kids I knew were at their peak, shining brightly, blossoming with newfound wisdom—I had to learn from a dog.

The matter was actually quite simple. I saw the animal at dawn, on my way back home. It had rained all night, the air was frigid and the road was pitted with puddles. The dog appeared from the darkness, paused near a car parked in front of the fried rice tent, looked around, approached the car's back tire, then lifted its leg—to piss, of course. I watched its urine spray out onto the tire. Some splashed onto the wheel well, the droplets sparkling in the streetlight.

The car door opened just as the dog was finishing. 'You pest!' I heard the driver swear.

Ah, I thought, even a dog knows how to make people mad. A dog forces people to acknowledge his existence, acknowledge his actions.

I was ashamed. I so rarely felt that other people were even aware of my existence—there were a few, but I was prejudiced against them. My shame deepened when I saw the driver kick at the dog, swearing, but he missed. 'You devil! You little rat!' Why couldn't I do the same? It was so simple. So easy. Then, I could annoy people, just a little, whenever I wanted. Make them mad, resentful, and even hurt, and in that way, finally, I would exist. It was never too late.

Full of humility and deep respect for all the dogs on the surface of the earth, I began pissing on all the bus stops I passed. I pissed on car doors, in faithful imitation. I pissed on security booths. Pissed on park benches. Pissed on the gates to the city hall.

'To the dogs, who taught me how to piss properly!' I yelled when, that night, at the height of my celebration, I pissed on the crates filled with apples and pears, which in just a few hours would meet the ripe lips of the ladies and gentlemen of the city. If there had been a drum, I swear I would have pounded on it, howling in celebration.

Just about every night I'd piss on a new corner of the city like a dog marking its territory—or like a cat? Whatever you prefer. I could rarely pee more than once in one night, even if I held it all night before I went to sleep, nor could I find a pickup filled with fruit every time, so I'd often just go wherever. From when I awoke in the wee hours until I returned home before daybreak, I'd be lucky if I'd been able to urinate twice.

Still, for the first time in my life, I fell asleep with my head full of plans. Where I would piss in the morning, where the morning after that, where next week. The world needed my faint aroma. Indeed, there wasn't much I could contribute to the wide world, let alone the alleyways of Stone Swamp, many of which I wasn't even familiar with, but at least in this little corner of the city, even if I died, I would have left my mark. Slowly but surely, I was not as useless as before. The world would be forced to acknowledge me.

The day after my creative expression up on the back of the pickup truck, I went in the afternoon to the fruit store. The truck was gone, and I saw piles of apples and pears in the boxes set out for display. Had they washed them first? Certainly not.

A young woman stood before the pears, a child at her side. She selected a few, put them in a plastic bag, placed the bag on the scale. A worker noted the weight, calculated the price, but before she tied off the top, the woman took one out.

That's right, take a nibble! Sample it! I almost yelled. Lick it. Bite it. Chew it. Swallow it. Just like the world had forced me to lick up all its bullshit, chew it, swallow all its bitterness.

Sweet lord, she was doing it! I saw her with my own eyes. She did take out a wet tissue and wiped the pear in her hand, as the child held the plastic bag, but I didn't care. I had pissed on it, and now she was biting into it, walking over to the cashier. Biting. Chewing. Swallowing. I imagined that a part of me, those few drops of piss that had escaped the wet tissue, were now coating her lips and her tongue.

This new pride I had in myself overflowed to the point that I realized: I used to be happy like this in the past, how had time slowly made me forget it? I should have been pleasing myself every now and then, these last sixteen years of my life.

I didn't think this feeling, or this behaviour was sick—at least, no more sick than the way most other people were. Everyone I'd ever met, they were all sick. I just had more self-awareness, and a greater sense of what I could do to get that joy in my soul.

Every night, lying on my lumpy mattress, I started daydreaming again, something I hadn't done for too long. If I were a cook in a food stall, I thought, I could easily stir one or two spoonfuls of my urine into the sauce. If I pushed a drink cart through the streets. If I worked as a household servant who could go in and out of my master's kitchen freely. If. If. If.

When would that pickup come again? It should come once every few days. I needed to start memorizing its schedule so that I wouldn't have to keep treading this path every morning. Then I realized I didn't have to stand straddling the bed of a pickup truck to piss on the full crates of fruit. Although I still considered that as the best way to do it, now I would piss at home, into empty mineral water bottles and then at night I could shower the shop windows without having to unzip my pants.

A few nights later I encountered the pickup again. I watched it arrive, from where I stood waiting at a nearby bus stop. Just as I expected, the driver and the young navigator got out, had a little stretch and wriggle in the parking lot, then both put cigarettes in their mouths and started walking east. I knew there was a coffee stall not too far away, that must have been where they waited till morning—the place had coffee and instant noodles and wooden benches that were useful if you wanted to lie down and doze off for a moment.

I did what I had done before. I had prepared two big plastic bottles of piss, and I poured it evenly out over all the crates. The smell made me nauseous—I'd had it ready to go for a couple of nights.

In the afternoon I went back to spy on whoever was buying the apples and pears. Sadly, I didn't see anyone eat anything with my own eyes, and this made me think—if what was raging in my mind could be called thinking—back to the dog, review the whole thing. As I did, the quite significant difference between us became clearer.

No wonder everyone thought I was a dummy, when something as simple as this had taken me days to figure out. When the dog had pissed on that car wheel, he'd made the driver feel sick, demeaned, and furious. Which was often how Father made me feel. And now what was I doing? I was pissing on bus stops. Pissing on house fences. Shop doors. But as soon as a new day dawned, the stench of piss was sent wafting into the air by the hot morning sun, or the agitation of the rain. When I pissed on fruit, people would only put it in their mouths the next day when the taste had faded, and the remnants might not even be recognizable. They'd eat it just like they'd eaten all that had come before. I wasn't upsetting them. I wasn't blessing them with feelings of humiliation, annoyance, or rage. I wasn't giving them anything except some urine—and they didn't even realize they'd received it.

I had lost. To a dog. No matter what, I would always lose.

Suddenly, I was exhausted.

All these weeks, while I was still thinking I'd never go back to school, I felt like I had the life I wanted. A life I could do whatever I wanted with. I sneered openly with scorn when I saw my friends leaving for school or returning home, as if to say, how tragic is your fate. Like lambs being herded to the pasture to feed, then herded back into their pen. But me? I was free to go anywhere. Free to return home whenever I wanted. Free to piss on anything. Freed from memorizing a history lesson, freed from calculating sums.

Mother still asked me, hopefully, every few days, 'When are you going back to school?'

'I don't know yet,' I'd say listlessly.

Just like everyone else, Mother suspected I was still grieving Father's loss. Grownups are actually that annoying—they answer their own questions just to mollify themselves. I was reluctant to just come out and say that I would never go back to school, that

I had no desire to meet with teachers who would remind me of Father—who, above all, would try to organize my life, telling me what I had to do and what I mustn't do. Honestly, I was reluctant to see other people, at least the people in this city. I had no desire to surrender my newfound freedom.

But surprisingly, it turned out it wasn't as easy as it seemed to avoid school for weeks, though at first I barely even noticed day turning to night and night to day. Every morning when I woke up I was assailed by the question, which bothered me more the more time passed: what am I going to do today? Even at night, as I lay there with my head on the pillow, the thought kept at me, 'What am I going to do tomorrow?'

That was when I'd walk around aimlessly, navigating the alleyways of our small city with my head bowed, looking at the ground, because I didn't want anyone to recognize me and try to engage me in conversation. I wasn't always successful, because someone always knew me from my clothes or my hair, and they'd ask 'Sato Reang, Umar's boy, what are you doing here?' I was forced to lie, and say something like, coming home from a friend's. To avoid that kind of thing, I would walk a different route every day. Sometimes I would even walk out past the settled areas, following footpaths that led me through gardens and fields, along rice paddies and through a small forest. I'd get tired out, and before the day had gone dark I'd return home to the same question, 'What will I do tomorrow?'

Staying at home wasn't a satisfying option. A few times a day my mother would call out, 'Sato, that's the call to prayer.' Ah yes it is, I should have replied, but I no longer pray! Yet even in this matter I couldn't speak frankly. I was too meek to face my mother. Of course she would never go snatch up a machete like Father had, or set my things on fire, but she would cry and I would feel sorry for her, and then I would blame myself, and then an evil thought would be born: would my life be better if Mother died, just like Father? So in the end I had to pretend to pray. At dawn, I'd awaken at the exact hour that Father used to bang on my bedroom door, leave the house, and pretend to be on my way to the mosque. Of course I didn't go there, I just sat at the pancake stall or walked along the beach watching the fishermen haul in their nets until morning light. And it was like that in the evenings too, I'd still leave the house so she'd think I was going to pray.

And then I realized: if I no longer lived in this city, I would be free from all this pretending. I'd be free from the pitiful expression on Mother's face. I could tell the world that I no longer prayed, I no longer fasted during Ramadan, that I was not a pious child, though my foreskin had been cut off and there was nothing I could do about it now. I could dedicate my life to worldly pleasures, and no one could stop me.

After thinking it over for a few more nights, which stretched out into almost two weeks, finally I decided to go back to school. I had a small plan for my future. Of course, Mother was happy. The school was also happy—they didn't make a fuss about these things. There was one upperclassman, a young girl who got pregnant out of wedlock. She'd disappeared from school for months, lots of folks thought she'd dropped out and gotten married. But soon after she had the baby—still not married—she came back to school. The principal just held her back a year because she'd missed so many months of instruction, so now she was in my class. Of course a few people gossiped, but the rest accepted her and considered the whole thing pretty normal. So that's why my situation of having disappeared for months after my Father died was a minor concern for our principal, and I immediately got my chair back in my class.

I arrived on Monday morning, as shy as a new kid. I had let my hair grow out, something that I'd never have done when Father was alive. I'd rolled my sleeves up twice, and I hadn't tucked in my shirt. I didn't have a knapsack, I'd just brought one notebook that I'd folded and stuffed into my pants pocket. That whole day, I muttered over and over that something had changed in me, and I wasn't who I used to be. That I was back at school not to learn, but to get a ticket out of this city, to get as far away from here as I could, if I could swing it.

Apparently Jamal didn't notice the difference. He came to me that first day, happy to see me back in school, and he said, 'Let's go to the mosque!' I almost howled in disbelief.

'ARE YOU A MEMBER OF DARUL ISLAM?' SATO REANG ASKED Jamal. The urge to bully and annoy the boy had flickered back to life. And it must be said, many of his classmates happily bullied those who seemed weak, especially kids who were no fun and kept to themselves.

That was when they started to watch porn videos, after having read all the cheap dirty paperbacks they could find. That was when they were starting to take hearty swallows of Orang Tua brand wine, share bottles of black beer, and hunt for the psychedelic mushrooms that grew in the piles of buffalo dung, so they could feel themselves swept away by a transcendental joy or terror. Some of them had been smoking cigarettes for a while, but now they had started to mix chopped-up dried datura flowers in with their tobacco.

For Sato Reang, this was when he finally started to feel like he belonged. He no longer needed to hide his face in his father's back when he passed by a group of them. He was there on Saturday nights. For the first time, he fought in the streets. He always remembered his virgin rumble—his nose leaked blood, but he knocked out the other guy's tooth and split his lip. He fought three more times in high school, which led him to a boxing gym. The instructor told him he wasn't talented enough to compete in the ring, but the practice would still be good for him. He was grounded for a week. If his father had still been alive, maybe he would have been beaten with a rod of rattan, or whipped with a stingray's tail. The most easygoing fathers used a ruler, or a leather belt—and it was no big deal, it happened to all the guys he knew, they displayed their scars proudly, like a collection of medals.

There was only one kid who never got any of that, and his name was Jamal, because Jamal never did anything stupid. He didn't want to do stuff like that, but it was more than that, he'd turn sickly pale in fear if one of the guys even tried to get him to make any kind of mischief. Just the fact that he didn't have even one ruler scar was enough for the other boys to look at him askance, like an alien creature.

'You don't want to watch some porn, Jamal? What, you afraid you'll have a hot spit shoved up your asshole right through your skull in the afterlife—that you'll get roasted in hellfire?'

Long after, when he ruminated on it, Sato Reang would think it would have been better if they'd just left that kid alone. Jamal had never made trouble with anyone. Usually he just sat on his bench, looking neat and tidy and polite. Sato Reang remembered how he'd button the shirt of his uniform all the way up, to the highest button. He was so shy, he'd stiffen up awkwardly if a girl approached him, you could see him struggling to breathe normally if she even just tried talking to him. He obeyed all the teachers, and took diligent notes in meticulous handwriting, with almost no cross-outs or mistakes.

'You really don't want to try this black beer, Jamal? All the guys have tried it. It tastes bitter, like horse piss. What, you're afraid in hell your mouth will be forced open and bubbling lava will be poured down your throat?'

Jamal looked at Sato Reang sadly, pitying him for how he'd changed. Sato Reang didn't care, and had no mercy. He'd already said, long before his father died, that he didn't want to be friends with Jamal.

'You're a coward, Jamal. A wimp.'

During break, Jamal would quietly slip out to the mosque on the corner of campus. Instead of gathering in the school canteen or fighting over a ball on the basketball court, he chose to pray or recite verse. And no one missed him, or even noticed he was gone. Sometimes he seemed more like a ghost—you'd think he was there but it turned out he wasn't, or you'd think he wasn't there but then he willed himself into existence. So when the bell signalling the end of breaktime rang out and he appeared, they got right back to tormenting him.

In fact, Jamal wasn't the only kid like that. There'd be one or two every year—when all the other guys decided to ditch school, they'd choose to be good boys and stay behind. When a girl threw a birthday party, they wouldn't attend or give her a present. In general, they were more pious than the other kids. They attended religious camp on school holidays, always joined the Friday service at school, and of course spent their recess in the mosque.

During the flag ceremony, these were the kids asked to lead the prayers.

Bullying Jamal mercilessly, Sato Reang found himself saying, 'What, are you a member of Darul Islam?'

At first, this was just another taunt—but when the guys saw how Jamal's expression changed, how his hands started to tremble, they started to really enjoy it. Following Sato Reang's lead, they started teasing him the same way.

Of course they'd heard about Darul Islam in their history lessons, though briefly. Darul Islam rebels. PKI, the communist party. The Permesta separatists. The secessionist Republic of South Maluku. None of the kids really knew what was the difference between any of these groups, just that they were insurgents and insurrectionists, and the Indonesian Army had squashed them all. Pancasila had been upheld. The Republic of Indonesia stood strong. If some kid farted in class, his classmates would curse him, 'You communist dog! You rotten Darul Islam louse!'

Sato Reang had heard stories about the Darul Islam rebellion from his mother's father. It wasn't some grand patriotic tale like the ones the veterans would tell and retell boastfully at every community gathering, because his grandfather was an ordinary farmer who just happened to live in an area that became a battlefield, in a little village between Garut and Tasikmalaya. His grandfather had even told him Kartosoewirjo, the great Imam of Darul Islam, and his entourage had once passed by. The villagers always made themselves scarce at dusk, because the night was gripped in the fists of the gangs—which is what they called the rebels. In the morning they would return to their settlement, because there were paddies and fields to tend to—with soldiers of the Republican Army on patrol, of course. The villagers read into that routine rotation symbolically, saying that Darul Islam was the darkness and the Republic was the light. Sato Reang was sure the other kids had heard the same stories, from their grandfathers or great-grandfathers.

At first they'd just been teasing Jamal about Darul Islam because he was so religious, and he always kept his distance. He was *other*, like someone who retreats into the forest.

Only later did Sato Reang realize that Jamal's expression changed, his hands trembled, for a reason. One Friday afternoon, a few soldiers from the Military Command office came to arrest Jamal's grandfather. This old man, whose picture Sato Reang had seen plastered on a banner when his family went on that 'picnic', had been using his Friday sermons to urge his congregants to stop saluting the flag. The flag was idolatry, that's what he said. After that little commotion, people began talking about Elder Scholar Ruhayat Jamil's past as a Darul Islam soldier—he'd fought on the slopes of Mount Sawal and been captured in the hills near southern Bandung. Luckily he hadn't had to face the firing squad, but he'd been thrown in jail for a few years.

That question upset Jamal more than any other taunt or tease, because he knew the follow up question was something like, 'Are you going to take up arms like your grandpa, Jamal? Raid the houses of humble farmers, and found an Islamic State?'

Jamal tried to avoid anyone who mocked him with that question; he would simply turn and walk away as fast as he could, but Sato Reang and his friends were really enjoying this new entertainment. They'd chase him down, corner him, and whisper, 'Are you sure you don't want to sin just a little bit, Jamal? Try a little black beer that tastes like piss? Or a porn video? You wouldn't have to pitch in for any of the rental fee, Jamal, you could watch for free. Oh, no I guess you wouldn't want to because you're a pious kid, pious like your grandpa. I saw you refusing to salute the flag on Monday morning. And I guess you were too lazy to sing the national anthem.'

The girls never joined in bullying him—they even protected him, pushing the guys away and screaming in their faces to leave Jamal alone.

But then, one day, in response to that question he'd been asked so many times before, Jamal spun around to face the boys who were teasing him, his eyes glassy. For a second, the boys thought it would end with a fight. But not so. Instead Jamal said, with pale trembling lips, 'Okay, sure. Who's afraid to watch some porn?'

Two nights later, nineteen guys crowded into one of their rooms. Jamal was sitting right in front, his face a foot from the television screen. They'd only rented one cassette, but they played it three times, and every time they watched mesmerized, their awkward laughter turning into heavy breathing. The next day, behind the bus terminal on the way home from school, Jamal agreed to try black beer. He opened his mouth wide, tossed back half a glass, and proclaimed it did indeed taste like horse piss. The guys all clapped. He drained the rest of the glass and they clapped harder.

This new Jamal who watched porn videos and drank black beer became the talk of the school, and the talk reached his mother's ears. She headed right for the office, where she erupted in tears of rage and complaint. The principal called the boys in, twisted their ears and gave them a stern talking to, which had absolutely no effect.

To celebrate, and, as Sato Reang put it, 'to welcome the participation of our Jamal, who is no longer pious,' they planned a party for the weekend.

Jamal had to pretend he was attending prayer recitation at some mosque so that his mother would give him permission to go out with them. All the guys pooled their pocket money. There would be plenty of black beer, and four chickens to be roasted, and the buffalo dung magic mushrooms.

That night they were beyond intoxicated. Everyone was puking in the grass, some of them puked on the roast chicken, but they still ate it. Four kids collapsed in the gutter and slept there, their chins and necks covered in dried vomit.

And Jamal? After emptying his stomach under an almond tree, he staggered into the street and whirled around, startled by the headlights of an oncoming car. The driver went for the brake but was so scared he pressed the gas instead. The car lurched forward, engine roaring, and slammed into Jamal. He was thrown into the air and then just lay there sprawled on the rocks.

Sato Reang froze. His friends looked at Jamal's body, expressionless for a moment, before erupting into curses and sobs and accusations. They brought Jamal's body back to his house. Everyone in the neighbourhood heard his mother's screams.

'He lived as a good boy for sixteen years. He knew what was right, but you all led him astray in a matter of days. Days! You scum! If he's going to hell, he's bringing all of you with him!'

The boys could not bear to stay at the house a moment longer. Not one of them went to the burial but soon after a few became pious, maybe in surrender or maybe out of true repentance. No one ever talked about it, not up until graduation day, but Sato Reang would never forget her screams. He carried them with him into adulthood, along with the sounds of a machete splitting open a plastic ball and the crackling flames devouring a small stuffed monkey.

'You scum! If he's going to hell, he's taking all of you with him!'

ALSO BY EKA KURNIAWAN IN SPEAKING TIGER

BEAUTY IS A WOUND

Eka Kurniawan

Described as *'One Hundred Years of Solitude* kicked into another gear', *Beauty Is a Wound* combines history, satire, family tragedy, legend, humour and romance in a sweeping polyphony. The novel begins with the Japanese occupation of Indonesia, then a Dutch colony, during World War II. Dewi Ayu, a beautiful half-Dutch, half-Indonesian girl, is captured by Japanese soldiers along with twenty others and brutalized. After the US Army frees Indonesia—and Dewi—from the Japanese, Dewi finds her family untraceable and their mansion occupied by American soldiers. Struggling to survive, she turns to prostitution and soon becomes the most sought after prostitute in the land.

Dewi Ayu gives birth to three daughters, each as stunning as herself. Over the course of their lives, Dewi and her daughters are beset by incest, murder, bestiality, rape, insanity, monstrosity, and the often vengeful undead. However it is Dewi's fourth daughter—named Beauty in a cruelly inverted joke—who draws them all together and brings this epic tale to its final conclusion.

Drawing on local sources—folk tales and all-night shadow-puppet plays, with their bawdy wit and epic scope—Kurniawan's gleefully grotesque hyperbole functions as a scathing critique of his nation's troubled past: the rapacious offhand greed of colonialism; the chaotic struggle for independence; and the mass murders of perhaps a million 'Communists' in 1965, followed by three decades of Suharto's despotic rule. Kurniawan's distinctive voice brings something luscious yet astringent to contemporary literature.

ALSO BY EKA KURNIAWAN IN SPEAKING TIGER

MAN TIGER

Eka Kurniawan

A wry, affecting tale set in a small town on the Indonesian coast, *Man Tiger* tells the story of two interlinked and tormented families and of Margio, a young man ordinary in all particulars except that he conceals within himself a supernatural female white tiger. The inequities and betrayals of family life coalesce around and torment this magical being. An explosive act of violence follows, and its mysterious cause is unravelled as events progress toward a heart-breaking revelation.

Lyrical and bawdy, experimental and political, this extraordinary novel announces the arrival of a powerful new voice on the global literary stage.

ALSO BY EKA KURNIAWAN IN SPEAKING TIGER

VENGEANCE IS MINE, ALL OTHERS PAY CASH

Eka Kurniawan

Translated from the Bahasa by Annie Tucker

Ajo Kawir and Gecko are lower-class Javanese boys in their early adolescence. Half-hearted students at the mosque down the road and curious about girls and sex, they spend most of their time riding their bikes and spying on fellow villagers in *flagrante.* Sent by his mother on a mission to bring food to Scarlet Blush, an old friend who has gone mad after the murder of her husband by some vigilante soldiers, Gecko discovers that the crazy woman is actually quite beautiful. He invites Ajo Kawir to spy on her with him one evening, and the boys end up witnessing her rape by two policemen. Deeply traumatized, Ajo Kawir is rendered impotent.

Despite his handicap, Ajo Kawir becomes one of the toughest fighters in the Javanese underworld, his fearlessness matched only by his unquenchable thirst for brawling. When he finally meets his match in the shape of the fearsomely beautiful bodyguard Iteung, Ajo is left bruised, battered and overjoyed—he has fallen in love. But will he ever be able to make Iteung happy if he can't make love like a man?

Vengeance Is Mine, All Others Pay Cash is a gloriously pulpy tale of bloody fists, broken hearts and duelling Jakarta truckers, from one of the most exciting and original voices in literary fiction today.